# Gracie's Tribe

# Gracie's Tribe

*Janice Naylor*

RED GERANIUM
BOOKS

Book design by the Troy Book Makers
Cover art by Michael Lewandowski

Printed in the United States of America

The Troy Book Makers • Troy, New York • thetroybookmakers.com

To order additional copies of this title,
contact your favorite local bookstore
or visit www.redgeranium.org

ISBN: 978-1-61468-312-4

5926

## Acknowledgments

Thank you to my editor extraordinaire, Sharon Beaudoin, for her questions and suggestions and for her tireless search for the wayward or missing punctuation. I appreciate your support, Sharon, and am truly grateful.

Thank you to my loyal readers who waited through a complete rewrite after the zip drive was destroyed and who continued to encourage me to persevere and complete this story.

# 1

## Kathryn

It was one of those cold, damp February mornings in the Northeast that can produce black ice on the roadways, a thin ice more treacherous than its obvious cousins because of its transparency. Kathryn lived in Troy, NY her whole life and was accustomed to driving in the hills of her hometown during winter. She had learned the hard way, and more than once, that black ice disguised as innocent and clear roadway could catch a driver off guard and send a car spinning out of control which is why she randomly tested the brakes of her old Reliant station wagon while following the slow morning traffic down the long Campbell Avenue hill.

When the line of cars stopped for the traffic light near Barna's Store, she took a few deep breaths to release the tension in her shoulders and then, as she did most mornings, turned her head to the right to peek at Burden's Pond tucked behind the store. A thin layer of ice had formed on the small pond overnight, covering it to the water's edge where a meringue of snow settled on the frozen lawn. A mirror image of the morning's bright blue sky and drifting white clouds reflected off the fragile surface of the pond. Most of the other drivers were oblivious to the natural beauty nearby, too distracted by the traffic light, revving their engines and calculating whether or not they would make it through the light before it turned red again.

Kathryn knew from experience that she wasn't going to make it through the intersection this time, there were too many cars ahead of her. She'd probably make it through the next time the light cycled from red to green. While she waited, she daydreamed, as she often did, about what the area looked like a century before. She imagined horse-drawn merchant carts and family buggies pulled by brindle horses maneuvering and bouncing over grooves in a frozen dirt road. She could almost hear Henry Burden's long gone water wheel, the largest and most powerful water wheel of its time, churning away and feeding water from the nearby Wynantskill waterfalls to Burden's Iron Works factory at the bottom of the hill.

Car horns beeping behind her jolted Kathryn out of her daydream and she stepped on the accelerator a bit too quickly causing the wheels of her old station wagon to spin on a patch of wet snow for a second or two before gaining traction and moving forward. When she reached the bottom of Campbell Avenue and pulled onto Fourth Street, she saw Annie's white Mercedes approaching in the oncoming lane. As usual, Annie wasn't paying attention to the road and it looked as though she was searching for something in the empty passenger seat as she sped by and up the hill. Kathryn gave a half-hearted beep from her car horn although she knew Annie was too distracted to hear. Annie was always distracted and Kathryn and all their mutual friends had given up trying to convince her to slow down

After a slower than usual drive to work Kathryn was relieved to arrive safe and sound at the parking garage a block away from her shop. She made her way over the newly shoveled sidewalks on Third Street until she was standing in front of the brownstone storefront. The brisk winter wind blew up her three-quarter length coat urging her to find the long skeleton key in her purse and unlock the front door. Stepping inside, her first official duty of the day was to turn up the thermostat and warm up the small space.

Each morning when she returned the old skeleton key to her bag, she was reminded of the bustling town Troy used to be when she was a child, before shopping malls became the next best thing. Before well-intentioned politicians decided to tear down a whole city block of Troy's turn-of-the-century buildings, including an old and elegant movie theater, and replace them with a scaled down atrium-fronted version of a mall. Unfortunately, the Atrium, as it was called, never became the shopping Mecca they had hoped for; instead, Kathryn watched as the Atrium became an empty memorial to bad judgment.

She also watched as many of her small business neighbors left Troy to move closer to the continuous stream of shoppers that marched in and out of the shiny new malls just a short car ride away. It never occurred to Kathryn to move her thriving business from Troy. She was convinced Troy was simply entering hibernation, and that it would re-emerge during some future spring.

In pleasant weather Kathryn would often close her shop and stroll along the city streets, walking to the Hudson River waterfront one block away. Childhood memories accompanied her, memories of walks with her mother on the same city streets, Kathryn's little white gloved hand folded into her mother's gloved hand as they joined the crowd of bustling shoppers on Saturday afternoons carrying the packages they collected as they moved from one store to the next.

On that particular morning, the black dial phone sitting on top of the antique glass display case began to ring as soon as the shop door closed behind her. By the time she reached it the ringing stopped but before she could hang up her coat in the small office in the back room the ringing began again. Kathryn assumed it was Annie. That Annie had heard her beep after all and was calling to apologize for not reciprocating.

"It's okay, Annie," Kathryn spoke into the heavy black receiver, "I could tell you were a million miles away." "Kathryn?" a man's voice spoke her name. "Yes?" she replied. "Kathryn, this is James, it's Grace; something terrible has happened."

# 2

## Caroline

Caroline hated that moment when consciousness crept in and obliterated the remnants of sleep. She struggled to will herself back to sleep but, as always, it was a losing battle. She lay on her bed waiting for her eyes to adjust to the morning sunlight streaming through the frosted windowpanes. Her head throbbed, her mouth felt as though it was filled with wallpaper paste and her esophagus burned from the abuse it suffered the night before. Slowly, hoping not to increase the pain in her temples, she turned her head to the left and was relieved to find that side of the bed empty. Too often she invited men home, strangers actually, that she met at the club or at some party.

Carefully she sat up and swung her legs over the side of the bed. She held that position until she felt confident that her legs would support her. After a few minutes she stood up, her right hand leaning on the cold marble of the table beside the bed. Again when she felt confident her legs would support her, Caroline walked across the large bedroom into the connecting bathroom suite. The thick white shag carpet felt comforting on her bare feet until the cold ceramic tiles on the bathroom floor sent a chill up her spine. She turned on the overhead heating lights and stood in their warmth as she undressed.

Caroline was disappointed, but not surprised, to see she was still wearing the beige cashmere sweater and beige wool slacks from the night before. She pulled the $300 sweater over her head and tossed it in a heap on the floor. Next she dropped her slacks to her feet, stepped out of them, and walked to the glass-enclosed shower where she opened the door and turned the hot water on full force. After a side trip to the medicine cabinet for three or four aspirin she slid off her beige lace panties and unclasped the matching lace bra letting it slide off her shoulders onto the floor before stepping into the hot stream of water.

She stood passively allowing the beads of hot water to bounce off her skin until the temperature of the water changed from hot to cold. Stepping out of the shower, she wrapped her slim body into a large, soft white bath towel before walking back to the bedroom. The frosted edges around the window panes reminded her of the frigid February weather waiting outside and she was relieved she had no reason to venture out into the day.

The room she stood in was filled with high-end furniture and expensive decorative pieces. The large room took up a small space in her huge and posh home. A home Caroline had stopped caring about a long time ago. Now it was just a place to crash; cleaned and cared for by people she hardly knew.

She dropped the towel to the floor and pulled open the doors to the walk-in closet that was filled with clothes from impulsive shopping sprees in New York City. Two unworn Chanel suits that were delivered six months before hung in front of her, still in their Bergdorf and Goodman protective bags. Expensive shoes lined the wall, all neatly stacked and color coded. Four or five fur coats, carefully draped on specialty hangers, waited at the far end of the long closet. "Stuff," as she called them, things she hardly noticed anymore. She grabbed the plain dark blue wool robe from the hook inside the door and was tying the belt around her waist when the bedroom phone began to ring.

She hated that stupid phone, a white porcelain replica of a 1914 French classic that her decorator had insisted upon. If she could work up enough enthusiasm, she would have it replaced. Who the hell would be calling me this early in the morning, she wondered and considered waiting until the ringing stopped and then taking the phone off the hook. Grabbing it, she barked into the receiver, "Yes!" "Caroline," Kathryn spoke gently, "I'm sorry to call you so early, but I have some difficult news to tell you. You'd better sit down." The tone in Kathryn's voice knocked the wind out of Caroline and she dropped into a nearby chair.

# 3

## Annie

Annie slid her Mercedes into a narrow parking space in the lot behind the Rensselaer County jail on Fifth Avenue, a white stone building with black bars on every window. She hated being late for appointments with clients. She believed her tardiness sent them the wrong message, and since they were only allowed one hour to meet with their attorney she had already wasted ten minutes of a 9:30 a.m. appointment, 15 minutes by the time she walked into the building. Her case earlier that morning at the Rensselaer County Courthouse just a few blocks away had been delayed. She thought she would have time to zip up Campbell's Avenue to Barna's store and buy a quick morning cup of coffee, but she ran into a grateful but talkative ex-client and now she would be running late for the rest of the day. Annie's friends kept telling her to retire. She didn't need the money and she always seemed to be squeezing 28 hours of work into 24-hour days.

Since graduating from Albany Law School twenty years before, Annie specialized in civil rights cases and even after all that time still felt the same anger and frustration every day as she tried to help the wrongly accused navigate through the legal mazes they faced. The poor guy waiting for her was a good example. A small mom and pop corner store had been held up in Lansingburgh, on the north side of Troy, and the perp showed a gun. When the owner resisted handing over the money from the cash register, the perp hit him on the side of the head with the weapon and fled. A half hour later, the police found her client two blocks away and arrested him for the attempted robbery and assault. The victim told the police he couldn't see the perp's face but described him as a small and slim man. Her client was a heavy set black man who happened to be in the wrong place at the wrong time.

Annie's parents, her dad a retired teacher and her mom a retired librarian, met while working at a high school in Harlem in the late 1930s. The importance and power of education had been drilled into their only child's head for as far back as she could remember, along with a sense of responsibility and pride in her heritage. After graduation from her neighborhood public high school in New York City Annie attended the State University in Albany, and then went on to Albany Law School. She grew to enjoy the relatively laid back style of upstate New York and after passing the bar exam decided to stay in Albany and hang out her shingle.

In the late 1950s, Annie and a few other Albany Law School alumni joined with area civil rights activists to form a legal advocacy group. Now, 21 years later, Annie was a senior partner in the well-respected law firm that evolved from that group and was still spending more than half her time on pro bono cases.

On that particular February morning, Annie rushed into the Rensselaer County jail stopping at the front desk to ask for directions. The police officer behind the desk handed her a pink message slip and told her the person who called asked that she return the call immediately, that there was an emergency. Her first thought was there was a medical emergency with her aging parents and then the fear that Dan might have been injured entered her mind. She was surprised to see Kathryn's name scrawled across the pink paper. She knew Kathryn wouldn't say it was an emergency unless something had gone seriously wrong, so she asked to use the black phone on the officer's desk and dialed Kathryn's number. After the phone rang a number of times Kathryn finally answered. "Kathryn, its Annie," she spoke into the phone. "What's going on?" "It's Gracie," Kathryn replied.

# 4

## Hedy

**P**ieces of sleet and freezing rain began to bounce off the bedroom window and woke Hedy from a sound sleep. An old habit kicked in and she quickly looked at the clock on her bedside table afraid she had overslept and would be late for work. Smiling, she sank back down into the warm bed pulling the soft down comforter to her chin as she remembered that as of three weeks ago she was a retired woman, no longer the Principal of School 16 in Troy's eastside. Before retirement she feared she would be bored staying at home but so far it seemed there were not enough hours in the day to accomplish everything.

Hedy had written a few academic papers during her career but always wished she had the time to collect the fragments of stories that formed in her head and write them down, perhaps finishing a novel one day. Now the days flew by as she sat at Christopher's desk in the den and wrote down those stories on long yellow sheets of lined legal paper.

She stretched and climbed out of bed, slipping her cold feet into the warm fleece-lined slippers Grace had given her the Christmas before. She zipped up her green wool robe with black bears marching in lines across the front, a purchase from a day trip to Lake Placid, and walked to the window to get a firsthand look at the weather. Below her a covering of crusted snow and ice was beginning to build on Fifth Avenue and she watched as a few cars drove by blazing a trail on the untreated street. Turning, she walked to the hallway and then down the old wood stairs, following the downstairs hallway to the large open kitchen in the back of the brownstone.

Hedy grew up in that house in downtown Troy. As a child, she and her friends walked up the hill to St. Paul's Catholic School every weekday morning and back down every afternoon. Most Saturdays they walked the few short blocks to the stores in downtown Troy where they spent their nickels at Woolworth's or Grants or any one of the wonderful old department stores that flourished in Troy when she was a kid. Most were gone now, out of business or moved out of town.

After high school Hedy was a student at Russell Sage College, not a mile from her parent's home. During her sophomore year she met Christopher who was an engineering student at Rensselaer Polytechnic Institute, a sprawling century-old university on the hilltop overlooking the city. They met at a frat party on a warm spring night. Christopher came to her rescue when she drank too much wine and went outside to sit on the concrete steps of the castle-like fraternity house on Second Street hoping the fresh air would make the world stop spinning.

Two years later, Christopher was a freshly minted engineer with a job waiting for him at Lockheed Martin in California and the ink was still wet on Hedy 's teaching diploma. They were married in St. Paul's Church on a beautiful August afternoon and after a large reception attended by family and friends; the newlyweds flew out of the Albany Airport toward the life they had planned together.

On that particular February morning, Hedy stepped into the warm kitchen and put on a pot of tea. She snapped on the radio and shuffled to the fridge where she opened the door and stared inside hoping something would inspire her to prepare a healthy breakfast. Eggs were simmering in a large frying pan on the stove when the phone rang. Hedy looked at the clock wondering who would be calling her so early, then lifted the receiver off of the gold colored wall phone. "Hello?" she said. "Hedy," Kathryn's voice spoke into her ear, "it's Gracie. There has been an accident."

# 5

## Grace

The sun was still below the horizon that cold February morning as Grace quietly slipped out of bed being careful not to disturb James, her sleeping husband. It would be another half hour before the girls woke and their morning chatter brought the house to life. Grace shivered in her long cotton nightgown and rushed to the small bathroom where her wool robe hung on a hook behind the door. She pulled up the wool socks she wore to bed the night before, slid her feet into the silly frog slippers the twins had given her for Christmas, and then quietly walked down the backstairs into the kitchen of the old farmhouse.

As usual, the kitchen was freezing and as she did every morning in the winter, Grace threw dried wood logs into the mouth of the big black potbelly stove, lit a match to the slivers of kindling, and closed the door. One of the first improvements they made after buying the farmhouse ten years earlier was to install a new state-of-the-art central heating system but the old kitchen was built over a crawl space rather than over the basement and was always cold in the winter until the heat from the woodstove began to circulate.

Like clockwork, as soon as the door on the woodstove closed, Lilly, their big lumbering black lab, plodded into the kitchen and stood waiting patiently by the back door. Grace walked over and tussled Lilly's ears, then opened the door letting the big dog out and frigid air in. Continuing her morning rituals Grace filled the large silver bowl with dry dog food from the 20 lb. bag behind the pantry door and topped off the matching water bowl. Most mornings Lilly was barking at the door ready to be let back inside by the time her bowls were filled, but not that morning.

Grace walked to the door and looked out the window. Lilly was 20 feet away standing in the snow in the semi-darkness. As she waited, Grace's mind began to wander to her father. She didn't like the sound of his coughing when she saw him a few days before and she made a mental note to stop by that afternoon and see how he was feeling. Then her mind flipped to the logistics of getting the girls to their after-school sports events and dance classes. Still concentrating on how to accomplish everything she needed to do that day and squeeze in a visit to Kathryn's shop; Grace absentmindedly opened the back door and let Lilly into the house, locking the door behind her.

Reaching down to pull a large pan from underneath the kitchen cabinet Grace felt a muscle twinge in her back. She straightened up slowly and promised herself, as she promised herself most mornings, that she would find time to take a yoga class, that she would eat better, and go to sleep earlier. At 34 years old, she was in pretty good shape but knew eating that extra brownie and staying up to read into the wee small hours of the morning were beginning to catch up to her.

She settled the pan into the kitchen sink and turned on the faucet. Her mind wandered back to her parents as she stared out the large picture window over the sink while waiting for the pan to fill. What if something happened to dad, (mom would be devastated), where would she live? If she was paying attention, instead of worrying about something that hadn't happened, Grace would have noticed the gorgeous pink and yellow streaks in the morning sky as the sun came up over the trees, but instead her thoughts were filled with responsibilities and demands on her time.

The pan, almost filled to the brim with water now, weighed a ton when she lifted it and carried it to the large country gas stove. She turned on the burner under the pan and walked back to the cabinets to retrieve five red plastic cereal bowls and matching cups. As she carried everything to the table the appointment calendar hanging on the wall caught her eye and she plucked it off and sat down at the kitchen table to develop a plan of attack for the day. Abigail, her ten-year old, had basketball practice after school until 4:30 and her six-year old twins, Kathryn and Dottie, had dance class that afternoon. How could she fit in a visit to dad and a stop at Kathryn's shop?

The next time she looked at the red plastic clock hanging awkwardly on the kitchen wall it told her James would be downstairs in a few minutes and the girls soon after.

Distracted and in a hurry, Grace walked to the stove and reached over the pot of boiling water for the box of oatmeal as she did every morning, but that morning when she brought the box to her, the sleeve of her robe caught the handle of the boiling pot of water and she watched as the pot made a small flip in the air before dumping the boiling water down the front of her. The scalding water hit her chest first, then slid down her stomach to her thighs and knees, finally forming a puddle on the top of her frog-clad feet.

Initially, Grace was surprised by how cool the hot water felt on her body, but a few seconds later a thousand nerve endings began to scream and James walked into the kitchen just in time to see Grace fall to the floor.

# 6

James ran to Grace's side. At first glance he didn't understand what had happened. Not until he saw the puddle of still steaming water surrounding her did it sink in that Grace had been burned. He picked up her limp hand and repeated her name over and over. "Gracie, Gracie, can you hear me? Gracie," he kept repeating. He was relieved when she tried to open her eyes, but quickly became horrified when he saw the pain registered there before her eyes closed again.

Dropping her hand, he ran to the old yellow phone on the kitchen wall and dialed 911. Averill Park was a small town and he and Grace knew every family that lived in the village. When Alice Donnelly answered his call, James screamed into the phone, "It's Gracie, she's been burned. Send someone right away." "James, is that you?" Alice responded. "Yes it's me," James screamed back. "Gracie is burned, send the medics right away." "OK, but tell me a few things first," Alice began. "How was she burned? Is she conscious?" "Water," James replied, "a pot of boiling water spilled down the front of her and no, she's not conscious and I don't want her to be, it's too painful."

"OK, James," Alice replied, concern and sympathy in her voice, "Johnny and Eddy are on call; I'll send them right away. In the meantime, don't try to remove her clothes. If it's cold where she is, gently lay a blanket over her and keep her warm until we get there."

James hung up the phone and was about to return to Grace when he noticed his three daughters standing in the kitchen doorway, their faces as white as ghosts. Startled, he turned to Abigail, the oldest, and told her everything was going to be okay, that mommy had an accident, and the medical people would be there shortly. Dottie began to scream and charge toward her mother. James caught her and put his broad arm around her small shoulders. "I know mommy looks bad right now," he told his children, "but we need to leave her alone and let her rest. Abigail, please take Kathryn and Dottie upstairs and play with them until I tell you it's okay to come down." The ever-skeptical Abigail agreed but gave her father the look that meant she didn't believe a word he was saying.

When he heard the children's footsteps heading up the stairs, James went back to Grace. She was moaning steadily and he could hardly bear to listen. He picked up her pale hand and began repeating to her that everything was going to be all right. He noticed the water was no longer steaming and wondered if Grace was warm enough. The skin on her chest had changed from a light pink to a bright red in the short time he had been gone from her side. He grabbed a roll of paper towels and soaked up as much of the water around Grace as he could before gently dropping a light weight blanket onto her small body.

It seemed like an eternity before he heard the sirens in the driveway. Gently dropping Grace's hand, he rushed to open the back door and followed the two EMTs across the kitchen. John knelt beside Grace to evaluate her condition. Ed took James aside and asked for details. A few minutes later John joined them and told James he had called Albany Medical Center and requested a medical helicopter to bring Grace to the hospital. "Is it that bad?" James asked, scared out of his wits. "I'm afraid so," John replied. It looks like second and third degree burns, maybe worse. We have to get her to the burn center quickly and the helicopter is the fastest way of getting her there. I've sedated her as much as I dare until a burn specialist can take a look at her. She is not in any pain right now."

James fell into the nearest kitchen chair. Ed asked if he was okay. "Yes, I'm okay," James replied, "I just can't believe this happened." "What about the children?" John asked calmly. "Is there someone you can call?" "Oh, the children," James sighed. "I'll call my sister Mary, she's right at the bottom of the hill and ask if she can sit with the children while we're gone." "OK," John replied. "While you're making those arrangements we'll prepare Grace for the trip to the hospital."

While waiting for Mary and the helicopter James went upstairs to talk to the children. He told them mommy was going to the hospital in a helicopter. The twins were thrilled at the prospect of a helicopter landing in their backyard. Abigail, on the other hand, looked more frightened than ever. Sooner than he expected, the sound of whirling helicopter blades passed over the top of the house and, along with the girls, he watched the helicopter land and the medics jump out of the sliding doors and rush toward the kitchen.

Giving each of his children a quick hug, James assured them their mommy was going to be fine and that Aunt Mary would take good care of them until mommy and daddy came home. Abigail clung to him while Kathryn and Dottie argued about whether the helicopter was blue or black.

By the time James arrived downstairs, Grace had been wrapped in a blanket, was on a gurney, and was being rolled outside. Mary walked up to the house as Grace went by and was clearly shaken when she reached James. "I can't talk now, Mary," James blurted out as he raced toward the waiting helicopter. "I'll call as soon as I can."

It took the loud rocking helicopter 15 minutes, including takeoff and landing, to cover the 13 miles between the farmhouse and Albany Medical Center. During that time James mostly prayed. He was afraid to talk to Grace, not wanting to wake her and throw her into physical pain, but also, not wanting to ignore her if his words were able to reach and comfort her. The EMTs spoke quietly to themselves as they monitored Grace's vital signs and James tried to read their faces for more bad news. As soon as the helicopter touched down on the roof of the medical center, a team of burn unit experts rushed out a side door and ran to the landing pad, ducking under the still-moving rotor blades.

James stared as they swiftly lowered Grace off the helicopter onto a gurney and was left watching their backs as they rushed her into the building. He had forgotten about John and Ed until Ed jumped out of the helicopter and helped James balance himself on the rooftop. "How are you doing, James?" John wanted to know. "Fine, I'm just fine," James replied knowing he was anything but. "There's nothing you can do right now," John continued. "You'll have to wait until the doctors evaluate Grace's condition." "Well I can stay with her, can't I?" James wanted to know. "No, afraid not," Ed responded. "You'll just be in the way." That's when James realized for the first time that John and Ed were guiding him through the building.

Grace was nowhere in sight when they arrived at the big glass doors, the words BURN UNIT printed in bright red ink across the front. Ed restrained James from walking inside, reminding him again he would just be in the way. Reluctantly James allowed himself to be steered to one of the orange faux leather armchairs in the waiting room nearby. After James sat down, Ed knelt on one knee in front of him. "Grace is with the best burn specialists in the area," Ed assured him. "It could take anywhere from an hour or longer before the evaluation is done." John's pager began to beep. "We have to go now, James;

the copter pilot is waiting for us. Do you have anyone you can call to stay with you?" "Sure," James replied, sensing that was what they wanted to hear. "Okay. Hang in there," were their parting words as they rushed toward the elevator.

For the next half hour James answered all of the nurses' questions and completed a stack of paperwork. When he was finished he returned to the uncomfortable orange chair and starred at the Burn Unit door for a very long time. So long in fact that the nurse behind the desk walked over and asked if he was okay. "Sure," James replied. "How about a cup of coffee?" she asked and when he nodded she added, "cream and sugar?" "No, thanks, black is fine," he whispered back.

"Now, don't forget you have your wife's bag there," she reminded him. "I do?" he asked, looking around the area. "In your hand," she said. As the nurse went to get coffee, James focused on Grace's bag. Looking inside, he wondered how Grace ever accomplished a thing. It was total chaos. Keys, bills, grocery receipts, tissues, a red wallet, eyeglass case, crooked sun glasses, and her small book of phone numbers with the Art Deco cover.

That small little book of numbers reminded James there were people to call. People who loved Gracie almost as much as he did, people who would never forgive him if he didn't call. Glad to have something to do, James walked back to the nurses' station and asked for directions to the nearest pay phone. The women took pity on him and slid a big black dial phone across the desk and told him to make as many calls as he needed.

The first person he called was Kathryn.

# 7

Kathryn hung up the phone and looked around her shop but all she could see were images of Grace in the helicopter and then in the Burn Unit at Albany Med. She called her husband, John. "Honey, a terrible thing has happened," she began. "Is it one of the boys?" John interrupted. "No, no, thank goodness, not one of the boys, it's Gracie. She's at Albany Med. Something happened in the kitchen this morning and she was scalded." "On her hand?" John asked. "No, much worse; according to James she's burned on more than 50% of her body." Kathryn's voice began to quiver. "Do you want me to come and get you?" John asked. "It's slow here at the hardware store this morning; I can close for an hour or so." "No, I'm okay," Kathryn assured him. "I'm going to make some phone calls, cancel this morning's classes, and then drive to the hospital."

A half hour later the calls had been made. Kathryn locked the heavy wood door to her yarn shop then rushed down Third Street and crossed Fulton Street to the parking garage. Normally she would have taken a few seconds to admire the Frear Building on the corner. Of all the architecturally stunning buildings in Troy, the

Frear Building with its magnificent three-story wrought iron staircase was her favorite, but this morning she didn't even see it.

If you asked her, Kathryn would not be able to tell you how she got to Albany Medical Center. She remembered driving on the Menands Bridge over the Hudson River and picking up Interstate 787, but her mind kept flashing back to the first time she saw Grace.

Kathryn's eldest son, Jack, had brought Grace and her brooding friend, Caroline, to their house one spring afternoon after school. She was working in the kitchen when she heard Jack's old jalopy speeding up the dirt driveway, kicking up stones and tossing them against John's work shed. Looking out the window over the kitchen sink she saw Jack bring the car to a stop, jump out from the driver's side, and run around the back of the car to open the passenger side door for the two young women.

Grace stepped out first. She was still wearing her school uniform, the gray blazer and red plaid skirt hung loosely from her small athletic frame. She was laughing at something Jack said and for Kathryn it was love at first sight. Grace stepped aside while Jack offered his hand to Caroline and helped her out of the car. Caroline was wearing the exact same school uniform as Grace but on her it looked more alluring, almost seductive with the red plaid skirt rolled up at the waist, bringing the hemline above the knee and the white uniform blouse opened just one button lower than her friend's.

Kathryn watched the threesome cross the front lawn and practically hop up the porch steps. Jack walked in the middle but there was something about the way he leaned in toward Caroline that told Kathryn her boy had a favorite. She listened as Jack pushed open the screen door on the porch and let it bounce against the door frame. As soon as they crossed the threshold, Jack yelled out, "Mom, are you home?" "I'm in the kitchen," Kathryn yelled back, and like a great breath of fresh air the three teenagers burst into the room.

Jack was a senior at LaSalle Military Academy, a private all-boys school in Troy, and now that they were closer she could tell the girls were younger. Each class in the Catholic school the girls attended wore a different color plaid skirt, but for the life of her Kathryn could never remember which class wore what. After introductions and bottles of soda were passed around, Jack and his friend Caroline excused themselves, Jack telling Kathryn he was going to show Caroline the small stream that ran through their property about a half mile from the house while Grace assured everyone she didn't really want to walk that far.

Kathryn was taken aback by Jack's obvious interest in Caroline. Aside from a few near misses, Jack never had a steady girl or seemed that interested in anyone in particular. He was tall and handsome like his father. He played football and basketball at school, was popular with his classmates, was an honor student, never missed a military ball, and was constantly invited to proms from other local high schools. Kathryn had a stack of bills for prom bouquets from local florists as proof. Yet, she sensed something different was happening between Jack and Caroline and was surprised when she eventually learned how long they had been seeing each other.

When the couple left, Grace turned to Kathryn and mentioned the knitting basket on the kitchen table. "Do you knit or crochet?" Kathryn asked. "No, I've never learned, but I'd like to one day." "Well, I've got time right now," Kathryn replied. "Would you like to start?" "Love to," Grace said with a wide smile on her face. And so their friendship began.

The memories faded as Kathryn pulled up to the ticket machine in the hospital parking lot. Albany Med was a research hospital and a huge building complex. On the few occasions she had been in the buildings before, she wandered around like a lost child until someone took pity on her and offered directions.

She parked her car as close as she could to the entrance, having no idea when she might leave to go home. As she walked through the automatic sliding doors, she worried about Caroline and prayed she'd drive carefully. The kind volunteer behind the counter gave Kathryn directions to the Burn Unit and Kathryn held her breath during the elevator ride to the fourth floor.

There was no one in the waiting room so Kathryn walked to the nurses' station and asked about Grace. The woman behind the counter told Kathryn that Grace was being evaluated, that two of their best burn specialists were with her; it would most likely be another half hour before there was anything to report and that James had just walked down the hall to the chapel.

# 8

Caroline dropped the receiver back on the hook, closed her eyes and tried to breath. Not Grace, she fumed, no, you cannot take Grace from me. Impulsively she walked to the fridge in her overpriced and seldom-used kitchen and yanked open the freezer door. She pulled out the Absolut Vodka and almost drained what was left in the bottle. Her mind was racing. No, this is impossible, she thought; this cannot be happening to me again.

The booze soothed her and she began to develop a plan. Albany Med, she told herself. I'll drive to the hospital. That's where her plan ended, but now she was a woman on a mission. She pulled on the first pair of jeans hanging in a long line of designer jeans in her well-organized closet. She slipped her bare feet into fleece lined boots, pulled on a black turtleneck cashmere sweater, grabbed her raccoon coat out of the hall closet, scooped the keys out of the crystal bowl on the table near the front door, and slid down the frosty front steps.

Her brand new 1980 silver Mercedes two-door coupe was right where she left it; buried half way in the snow bank surrounding the U-shaped driveway in front of the turn-of-the-century Greek revival home her late husband had loved so much. She, on the other hand, could care less about the house. Occasionally she thought she would be perfectly content in a condo somewhere rather the big old house on Pinewoods Avenue, but she never worked up enough enthusiasm to do anything about it. She just didn't give a damn.

She was proud of herself when she drove by the liquor store on Pawling Avenue but had no resistance a mere ten minutes later when she pulled into the parking lot of the liquor store on busy Route 9 in Latham. In no time she was back behind the wheel driving down Route 9 toward Albany with a newly opened bottle of Absolut balanced on the control panel between the front seats. By the time Caroline pulled into the parking lot at Albany Med, the Absolut was a quarter empty and she was feeling very much in control although the nurse that Caroline barely missed running over in the parking lot might have begged to differ.

Without paying much attention, she pulled into an empty parking space and turned off the ignition. She dropped her head against the leather headrest and closed her eyes. She wasn't like the rest of them, she thought. It wasn't easy for her to walk into the hospital, she couldn't be helpful and say the right words and do the correct thing when her heart was breaking.

Gracie was her best friend. They met in third grade at Sacred Heart School six months after Caroline's parents were killed in a car crash and her world fell apart. Caroline was a shy little girl living in the Griswold Heights Apartments with her mother's unmarried sister, Ida. Caroline loved her Aunt Ida. Aunt Ida bought her anything she asked for with the interest from the trust fund her parents had left for her Their apartment was always well kept, clean clothes filled her closet and dresser, and healthy food was always in the fridge. But, Aunt Ida had problems of her own and came home from work each day with a six pack of beer.

Grace lived with her parents in a small cottage on Excelsior Avenue near Sacred Heart School. The girls met at Kinloch Park during a school lunch period. Grace was playing with friends on the swings when she noticed Caroline leaning against the metal park fence watching them. Without hesitation Grace walked over to Caroline and asked her to push her on the swing. At first Caroline declined but Grace insisted and from that moment on they were fast friends.

They spent most weekends sleeping over at each other's houses. During the summer they were off to the park or played hopscotch and jump rope on the sidewalk. Then they'd either strap on their roller skates or jump on their bikes and go to a corner store where they'd fill small brown paper bags with penny candy. In the winter, they held hands as they skated on nearby Belden's Pond and laughed at each other when the neighborhood boys snatched their knit hats from their heads.

They liked spending time at Caroline's apartment because Aunt Ida fell asleep early on the recliner in front of the TV and they were left to their own devices until morning. They selected random people from the phone book and called them late at night, giggling and rolling on the floor when someone answered. They ate as much as they wanted and watched whatever they wanted on TV. They balanced books on their heads for hours after watching the Miss America Pageant each September and played the latest 45s on Caroline's portable record player until they couldn't keep their eyes open any longer.

Grace was with Caroline the first time she met Jack. They were 11 year old seventh graders and he was a good looking and cocky 14 year old freshman cadet at LaSalle high school. Grace and Caroline had walked to Fitzies store across from their school and Jack and some of his friends were sitting on the metal railing outside. When they saw Grace and Caroline they jumped off the railing and stepped in front of them, blocking their way. The boys thought it was all very funny, but Grace was not amused. Caroline, on the other hand, kept peeking at the tall handsome boy in the white shirt opened at the collar wearing the gray military uniform pants with black stripes down the sides.

The boys eventually got bored and let them pass, but when they came out of the store, Jack was waiting for Caroline. Jokingly he gave her a dime and told her to call him when she was older. After that first meeting Caroline and Grace saw Jack occasionally hanging around with his friends at Fitzies, but it wasn't until the winter before

Grace and Caroline started high school that they talked again.

It was a cold winter evening. Grace's parents dropped the two girls off at Belden's Pond, the city-run outdoor skating rink where lots of their friends spent the weekends. Although they had skated there many times during daylight, Grace's parents finally gave in and allowed her to go skating at night for the first time now that she was in eighth grade. The two friends felt very grown up indeed.

After climbing down the 50 rickety and jagged wood steps that led to the large rink where the snow had been cleared off the frozen pond, they stopped at the small warming shed and joined the crowd of skaters sitting on long rustic wood benches who were putting on or pulling off their skates and depositing or collecting discarded boots that were stored in the small cubbies near the crackling potbelly stove.

Outside the night was magical. It was crystal clear. A full moon balanced overhead surrounded by twinkling stars. The bare light bulbs strung around the perimeter of the rink might just as well have been sparkling chandeliers as far as the two starry eyed friends were concerned. When they reached the edge of the rink, they hung on to each other while they removed their skate guards and then pushed off onto the ice.

Younger kids sped by forming a long chain of skaters holding on for dear life. Boys and girls from their class yelled hello as they flew by, chasing each other on the ice, their laughter hanging in the frigid night air, their breath captured in long white streams of vapor. In the center of the ring, girls whose families could afford to pay for figure skating lessons jumped and spun in ways that made Grace and Caroline jealous but the two friends looked at each other and said, "show offs" at the same time which made them double over laughing.

Grace didn't notice Jack until he was skating beside Caroline, but Caroline noticed him as soon as she stepped on the ice. Jack said something to Caroline that made her laugh in that wanting-to-impress-this-guy sort of way and Grace rolled her eyes. Grace was glad when Jack skated away and Caroline pretended nothing special had happened.

Throughout the night pop songs were played over the loudspeaker, music the girls hardly noticed until it was announced that it was time for a couples skate and everyone was asked to leave the ice. As the first bars of Sam Cooke's "You Send Me" began to play, Jack appeared and held out his hand to Caroline. She, of course, declined because a really good friend would not leave her best friend standing alone but Jack did not give up and in a flash he was back dragging a classmate who agreed to skate with Grace and off they went, Jack and Caroline chatting away in front while Grace and the unnamed volunteer skated quietly behind.

And so it began …

# 9

Hedy sat at the old Formica kitchen table that gray morning and watched the room darken. Who knows how long she might have sat there had the sun not broken through the clouds and streamed through the two six-foot high kitchen windows. The bright light stirred her and without thinking too much about it she marched back upstairs to her bedroom and pulled a well-worn brown sweat suit out of the closet.

She dressed, tied on her Nikes, and walked out of the brownstone toward her little Honda parked in front of a house a few doors away. She began to complain to herself about the atrocious parking situation in the city, especially when it snowed. She didn't realize until she arrived at her car that she hadn't thought the plan through. She stood there with no coat, no boots, no gloves, and no car keys, looking at the window scraper on the back seat of the locked car. That's when she realized she was sobbing.

Turning, she walked back to her house, up the old porch steps, through the front door that she had left wide open, through the little foyer and right into the parlor where she threw herself on the dark green suede sofa and had a proper cry. Five minutes later she felt better.

A half hour after that she had taken a long hot shower, dressed in a decent pair of black slacks and a black v-neck sweater, even managed to throw a colorful black and red scarf around her neck. Boots, coat, keys, gloves; she checked them off and was prepared for the weather the second time she stepped outside that morning.

Hedy first met Grace at Kathryn's kitchen table. Kathryn had been coaxing Hedy to learn to knit and eventually Hedy gave in and agreed to one or two lessons. In retrospect, Hedy suspected she was a part of a grand plan Kathryn had spun; introducing Grace, the newly minted teacher, fresh out of Russell Sage College, to Hedy, the experienced newly minted school principal, also a Russell Sage alumna.

Hedy was all thumbs and watched in awe as Grace conquered every challenge Kathryn laid out for her. The evening ended with Grace taking home a half finished pink scarf and Hedy leaving with a half-used ball of yarn and encouraging pats on the back from Kathryn.

They both returned to Kathryn's the following week; Grace with a lovely knitted pink scarf draped around her neck and Hedy with her half-used ball of yarn. When Hedy lamented about how little progress she had made during the week, Kathryn commented innocently that, well, after all, Grace has lots of time to practice since she is just sitting at home every day sending out her resume, hoping to find a teaching position. Her comment went right over Grace's head, but Hedy, who knew Kathryn longer, shot her friend a "really, are you kidding me?"

look when she recognized that she had fallen right into Kathryn's trap.

Two weeks later Grace and Hedy sat in Hedy's office at School 16 talking about an opening for a substitute teacher and Grace's expectations for her future. Hedy couldn't help but like the sweet 21-year old sitting across the desk from her: so bright, so honest, so spanking new. Listening to Grace, Hedy was reminded of how enthusiastic she had been when she was hired for her first teaching job. The hours she spent every night developing instruction strategies, looking for relevant photos to cut out of Life Magazine and paste on large pieces of cardboard hoping to spike the children's interest while her new husband, Christopher, sat nearby reading in the warn-out recliner in their first Sherman Oaks apartment. If she had known then how limited their time together would be, she would have followed the suggested lesson plans and spent that precious time with Christopher.

Looking at Grace, her eyes sparkling, her expressive face telling the story before the words spilled out of her mouth, Hedy recalled the times many years before when she couldn't contain her own enthusiasm for teaching and she caught veteran teachers rolling their eyes at each other when they thought she wasn't looking and then, not that many years later, Hedy was the veteran teacher rolling her eyes at the enthusiastic new substitutes.

Hedy hired Grace that very morning. She knew enthusiasm was exactly what her worn out teaching staff needed and she wanted to snap Grace up before another school found out what a treasure she was. Now her treasure was unconscious somewhere in the huge brick building she could see in the distance.

Hedy pulled into the Albany Med parking lot, accepted the ticket from the automated parking attendant, and backed her Honda into the parking spot next to Caroline's silver Mercedes. She was only half-surprised to see Caroline still in the car, her head tilted back on the headrest, her eyes closed. Any other morning Hedy would have knocked on the car window but not today. She had no patience for Caroline's bad girl behavior that morning.

# 10

Annie hung up the phone and leaned against the front desk. When the officer looked at her with a puzzled look on his face, she signaled she was okay, then asked "One more call?" She called her office and asked her assistant to cancel all appointments for the rest of the day. The client she had come to meet that morning had already waited 15 minutes so she put on her big girl boots and marched into the small conference room gushing apologies and trying to stay focused. Forty-five minutes later Annie was in her car and heading over the Congress Street Bridge into Watervliet on her way to Albany Med.

Grace and Annie met on a hot July evening in 1963. They often laughed about how they met; especially if Annie told the story.

Annie was guest speaker at an impromptu meeting of local civil rights activists held in the sanctuary of St. Joseph's Roman Catholic Church in South Troy. The purpose of the meeting was to organize a bus trip to Washington, DC, and participate in an August 28th Civil Rights March organized by Rev. Martin Luther King. Approximately 30 people were in the sanctuary, most were representatives of local African American groups.

There were a few white faces sprinkled in the mix. The hope was to get a minimum of 100 local people to make the trip to DC and although Annie was a tiny woman, just 5' 2 and 120 lbs., she had a large personality and had no problem reigning in the discussion when it wandered off topic.

That is until she saw the young woman with the blue hair.

As the meeting continued, the sun dropped lower in the sky until a final ray streamed through one of the church's dark blue Tiffany windows, settling on the young woman in the back as though she was a pot of gold at the end of a rainbow and turning her sun-streaked blonde hair powder blue.

The sight stopped Annie mid-sentence. The young woman was a reporter for a local high school paper and continued scribbling notes into the black and white Composition notebook she was balancing on her lap. Most people followed Annie's gaze and were struck by the moment. When the girl noticed the conversation had stopped she lifted her head to see what was happening and was shocked to find everyone looking in her direction. She looked over her left shoulder to see what was attracting so much attention. Finding no one behind her, she turned around to a sea of smiling faces. "What? What did I do?" Grace sincerely wanted to know.

"You didn't do anything, Sweetie, but I think you're having a religious experience. Either that or we are."

Everyone laughed congenially and Annie explained to the young woman what had happened.

Annie noticed the blue-haired girl hanging back after the meeting and hoped she didn't have too many questions. It had been a long day and she was anxious to get home. "I'd like to sign up for the bus trip to Washington," Grace stated matter-of-factly. "How old are you?" Annie asked. "17," Grace said proudly. "You have to be 18 to come with us," Annie replied thinking that would end the discussion. "What if I get a release signed by my parents?" "Well, I guess that would be okay, but you need to understand that this march could be dangerous. Lots of people do not want this to happen and a blonde girl like you is going to stand out in the crowd." Annie told her frankly. "I'm not afraid," Grace replied, a look of determination on her face. "Maybe you should be." Annie smiled back.

"What's your name?" "Grace, Grace O'Donnell." "Well, Grace O'Donnell, I'll tell you what, you send a release to me at the address on this business card, signed by your parents, and I'll send you the details of where you can get on the bus. Okay?" Grace stuck out her hand, "We've got a deal," she said. "Oh," Grace added as an afterthought, "I'm sure my friend would like to come also." Exhaling, Annie told her, "Okay, but your friend's parents also have to send me a signed release."

Two weeks later the signed release form from Mr. and Mrs. O'Donnell was in Annie's office mailbox. Damn she thought as she opened the envelope. I can't believe her parents are willing to let her go.

At midnight on August 27, 1963, three yellow school buses sat in front of the Cathedral of the Immaculate Conception on Eagle Street, in Albany, a half block away from the Governor's Mansion. Small groups of marchers spoke quietly and walked toward the waiting buses, the shadows of scaffolding and cranes towering overhead. They were surrounded by the remains of blocks and blocks of neighborhoods that had been demolished, their occupants displaced, when New York State enforced eminent domain to claim 93 acres in the middle of the city of Albany to build then-Governor Nelson Rockefeller's South Mall, a complex of state office buildings, theaters, art galleries, and museums.

Annie checked off names as people climbed onto the buses. There was an air of camaraderie tempered by a solemn sense of purpose. As the checkmarks grew on the list on her clipboard, Annie was aware of the empty box next to Grace O'Donnell's name. During the previous months, she had spoken to Grace and her father about the trip and ended up making a personal commitment to Grace's dad that she would keep an eye on Grace and her friend after it became obvious that Grace would not be deterred. Now it looked like that was a non-issue.

Annie greeted the last of the arrivals and was walking toward the buses when she heard a car squeal to a halt behind her. She just knew it was Grace. Turning around she watched Grace kiss the driver behind the wheel of the big black Buick goodbye before she rushed out of the passenger side of the car balancing a platter with a Tupperware cover. Mr. O'Donnell stepped out of the driver's side of the car and looked directly at Annie. Annie understood his unspoken concern and smiled at him then whispered, "I'll take care of her." He nodded and climbed back into the car where he would wait until the buses pulled away.

When everyone was accounted for, Annie and Grace climbed on the bus and claimed their seats, while Grace chatted about her friend Caroline explaining she would not be coming, something about a boy. As soon as they sat down, Grace removed the Tupperware cover from the platter she was holding revealing dozens of Toll House chocolate chip cookies she had made for the trip. Immediately Grace turned around and handed the platter to the couple behind them directing them to help themselves and pass it along. Those cookies became Grace's trademark. As time went by Annie and Grace walked side by side in one civil rights march after another and everyone knew Grace and Annie were on the bus when the platter of Toll House cookies was passed around.

It turned out that the August 28, 1963 March for Jobs and Freedom was the largest political rally Washington, DC had ever seen. Somewhere between 200,000 and 300,000 people attended that rally and, in that record-setting crowd, Annie and Grace, their arms locked, stood just 100 feet away from the Lincoln Memorial while Martin Luther King delivered his iconic "I Have a Dream" speech.

Memories of those times with Grace vanished in a puff of smoke when Annie pulled her car into the Albany Medical Center parking lot. She passed the cars of her friends, Kathryn, Caroline, and Hedy and pulled into the first available space. Unlike her friends, Annie knew the medical center well having spent many an hour waiting for a client to be pieced back together. After stopping at the information desk, Annie stepped into the elevator and, like her friends before her, held her breath until the elevator doors opened at the Burn Unit.

# 11

The first touch was so gentle on their shoulders neither of them felt it, but Kathryn saw a movement in the silent chapel and turned to find a nurse from the Burn Unit standing behind them dressed in a crisp white uniform, a starched white cap positioned carefully on her brunette curls. "Mr. Stephens," the nurse whispered. "The doctors have finished their evaluation of your wife and would like to speak with you now." Panic, hesitation, and finally resignation washed over James' face before he slowly stood and, with Kathryn by his side, followed the nurse down the long foreboding corridor.

Back at the Burn Unit waiting room a tall young man in a white medical jacket stood near the nurses' station reviewing a medical chart. As soon as the nurse spoke to him he turned around and stretched out his open hand to James. "Mr. Stephens, I'm Dr. Watson." James and Kathryn both raised their eyebrows involuntarily. "I know, I know" the doctor conceded with a faint smile on his young face, "please don't hold it against me. Let's sit down," he suggested as he directed James and Kathryn to a small grouping of chairs. "Are you Mrs. Stephen's mother? He asked Kathryn. "No, a friend," she replied.

"Are you comfortable with your wife's friend listening to this conversation?" he asked James. "Of course," James responded.

"Your wife has some very serious burns, Mr. Stephens," he began. "She has burns over what appears to be 55% of her body. She has suffered first, second, third, and perhaps even a fourth degree burn on her right knee. Here's a brief explanation of what that means: Her shins and lower arms appear to have suffered first degree burns; the burn is painful, but not serious. With a first degree burn, the injury is to the top layer of skin. Her lower arms will blister but should heal without too much attention. There appear to be second degree burns on her stomach and both thighs; deeper layers of skin have been injured.

Third degree burns are more serious and she has suffered those burns on her upper arms, chest, abdomen, and the tops of her feet. Third degree burns go even deeper into the skin layers and nerve endings are destroyed. Because the nerve endings have been destroyed those areas may not hurt at all, but the surrounding healthy areas will be painful.

Now, let me explain what's going on with her knee: if it is a fourth degree burn, not just the skin layers have been damaged, but there will be damage to the underlying muscle, tendon, and ligament. We're not sure if it is a fourth degree burn, it's too early to tell yet." Dr. Watson stopped talking to let the two crestfallen people sitting before him catch their breath.

James had been swallowing the question for hours and was surprised when it was the first question that came out of his mouth, "Will she live? Is Grace going to die?"

Dr. Watson's demeanor became more serious. "Right now, Grace is sedated and comfortable. She is getting fluids and antibiotics via IVs. The nurses are cleaning and dressing her wounds. What we are immediately concerned about is her breathing. It is not uncommon and actually likely that a person with Grace's injuries will develop breathing problems. We also have to watch for signs of shock. Within the next 24 hours we will begin skin graft procedures. The sooner we start, the better. I will remove the injured skin and replace it with a layer of healthy skin. Right now Grace's body is responding to the injuries as expected but I would be doing you a disservice if I did not reinforce how serious her status is. With these types of injuries, her condition could change very rapidly."

Again, Dr. Watson stopped talking and it seemed to him the two people in front of him had sunk lower into their chairs. As the minutes ticked by, it became clear they were having a difficult time processing the information he had just given them. That's enough for now, he thought and decided to hold additional information about Grace's condition for later. "I'll tell you what," he said as he stood up and interrupted the silence, "I'm going back inside. In ten minutes or so I'll return, and you can ask me any questions you may have. Okay?" James and Kathryn nodded in unison, reminding him of the Roger Maris and Mickey Mantle papier-mâché bobble head dolls he had seen in the back window of a car on his way to the hospital that morning.

Hedy had entered the waiting room in the middle of Dr. Watson's explanation and, not wanting to interrupt, she slid into a chair on the periphery where she could hear every word. Like her friends, her mind had frozen and she was unable to pull two thoughts together. Seeing Hedy sitting there was the diversion that Kathryn needed to click back into gear. She stood up and walked to her, took her hand, and hugged her. They walked together back to James and pulled two chairs forward to circle around him. James was sobbing and there was nothing to be done but let it run its course.

Suddenly a woman's voice shrieked: "OH NO, SHE'S GONE ... GRACE IS GONE." They all snapped their heads around and saw Caroline standing 8 feet away on the verge of collapse. At that moment the elevator door opened and Annie stepped out just in time to catch a swooning Caroline before she hit the floor.

# 12

Before he had a chance to talk with James and Kathryn again, Dr. Watson was called away to another emergency. Dr. Devan, his partner in their medical practice, stepped in to conduct the second meeting with Grace's family. Dr. Devan was older, could have been Dr. Watson's father. He was tall and slim and attractive. Not movie star handsome but attractive in the way of men who were gawky teenagers but grew into their looks and developed an appealing self-effacing charm over the years.

By the time Dr. Devan walked into the small waiting room, it was almost filled to capacity with people concerned about the only patient in the Burn Unit that morning. He walked to the waiting faces, introduced himself, and explained Dr. Watson's absence. "I'm sure you have questions," Dr. Devan began as he sat in the only empty chair.

"How is she?" James started. "She's okay," Dr. Devan began, "She's not in any pain" he continued and thought he heard a group sigh of relief. "Her vital signs are responding normally to the types of burns that she has suffered. She will continue to receive fluids for at least the next 24 hours because these types of burns damage blood vessels and can cause fluid loss which can lead to hypovolemia, which simply means low blood volume. She suffered from hypothermia, which means her body temperature dropped to a very low level because her injured skin could no longer do its job and her body was losing heat faster than it could produce it. We have addressed both of those problems and she is responding well to the therapy."

"Right now our biggest concern is bacterial infection," he continued, "so far so good. It's a delicate balance of keeping the wounds clean as we begin skin grafts and continue treatment. Dr. Watson and I discussed his earlier conversation with you and for all practical purposes, her condition has not changed."

"Dr. Watson mentioned that Grace's breathing could become an issue," Kathryn began. "How is her breathing now?" "A bit labored, but we suspect that has more to do with the stress her body is experiencing right now rather than the burns themselves. People who have been in a fire with heavy smoke often suffer from burns in their lungs but she has been spared that at least. We are monitoring her regularly for any potential breathing problems," Dr. Devan replied.

James asked about her knee. "Dr. Watson thought there may be fourth degree burns on one of Grace's knees. What are the consequences if that proves to be true?" Dr. Devan took a breath and began, "Fourth degree burns not only affect the skin, but also the muscle and ligaments below. There may be permanent damage to the joint."

"But it can be treated, right; physical therapy, other options?" James asked. "Let's not go down that road yet," Dr. Devan replied. "We have some miles to go before we need to think about those options. It will be a few days before we're sure of the damage to her knee." James was not happy with the doctor's response, but also not ready to hear more so he let the conversation end.

Dr. Devan sat quietly for a few moments, looking at the group before him. Over the years he had observed how stress and anxiety change a face. He had walked right by family members after their loved ones were on their way to recovery, not recognizing their softer, less troubled faces. However, fear and tension were written all over the faces before him now.

During the 30 years he had been practicing medicine, Dr. Devan had developed an expression he used when dealing with the friends and families of his patients. Some patients had no one, some just a few, but the lucky ones had what he referred to as "a tribe." This woman, what was her name, he wondered, "ah yes, Grace," had a tribe and from that moment on Dr. Devan would refer to James, Kathryn, Annie, Hedy and Caroline as "Gracie's Tribe."

# 13

Before he left Gracie's Tribe, Dr. Devan told James he could go in and spend a few minutes with Grace but told the women that he was sorry they could not, due to the need to be vigilant against possible infections.

Dr. Devan walked with James and quietly explained what to expect. "Your wife is sedated and sleeping. She will not respond to you in any way. She has a few IV tubes, one for liquids and the other is antibiotics. Your natural instinct will be to reach for her hand, but please do not touch her; again, we need to keep her as germ free as possible. Her wounds are bandaged and she is covered with a small tent that prevents anything from lying directly on her chest. You will see her face has not been affected and her hands are slightly pink. The nurse will ask you to leave after a few short minutes and my advice is that you go home and get some rest." James began to protest, but the doctor insisted. "Not only go home now, but there's no need for you to come back this evening. She will still be in a deep sleep and you won't be able to spend more than five minutes with her. I know it's hard, but you need to rest and take care of yourself so that you will be able to be there for her when she truly needs your help. If anything happens that you should know about, you can be sure we will call you no matter what the hour."

By the time Dr. Devan stopped talking, they were standing in a small office inside the Burn Unit. The doctor helped James dress in a sterile medical robe, tied a matching blue mask around his mouth, and then led him to Grace's bedside. James' first reaction was relief, In spite of all the tubes and medical paraphernalia surrounding her, Grace looked peaceful. Her face looked exactly the same. He began to question if he had overreacted. He began to think that perhaps the injuries were not as bad as he imagined.

"I'll leave you now," the doctor said to James, patting him on the shoulder. "Either I or Dr. Watson will see you in the morning." Turning to the nurse he said, "No more than five minutes, please." She nodded from the place where she stood slightly behind James, prepared to support him if his legs gave out, something that happened often in the Burn Unit.

Returning to the waiting room, Dr. Devan told the rest of Gracie's Tribe to go home, that James would also be going home, and there was nothing to be done now; then he left. After brief discussion it was decided they would wait to get a report from James and then Kathryn would take him home.

James looked much better when he walked through the door from the Burn Unit. "She's sleeping and, other than the bandages, she looks good," James reported. Everyone breathed a sigh of relief because they all wanted to believe James' more sanguine version of Grace's condition rather than the doom and gloom doctor reports.

Like a pack of weary children, they reluctantly gathered their overcoats, hats and gloves and headed to the elevator together. James stopped at the nurses' station to be sure they had his correct phone number and Kathryn pulled Caroline aside and asked if she needed a ride home. "No, I'm fine," Caroline insisted, buoyed by what she perceived as good news from James.

It was early afternoon when Kathryn dropped James off at his old farmhouse. The morning had turned into a gray and dank afternoon and the ice in the driveway was covered with a layer of melted snow making it treacherous to walk. It was so slippery underfoot that Kathryn waited in the car to be sure James made it to the kitchen door.

When James opened the door and walked inside he was almost knocked over by the twins. "Hi daddy, where's mommy? Did you get us anything at the hospital? Why didn't you come home in the helicopter? Do you think we can take a ride in the helicopter? " they gushed. He knelt and took them both in his arms. "Wow, you two have lots of questions," he started. "Where's mommy?" Kathryn wanted to know. "Mommy is staying in the hospital for a few days," he said. "When is she coming home? She promised to take me to Nancy's party on Saturday." Mommy won't be home by Saturday, honey, but we'll work something out, we'll get you to the party."

James looked around for Abigail, but she was nowhere to be found.

# 14

Annie drove slowly alongside the narrow creek that tumbled by her old stone colonial house. She was emotionally and physically exhausted. Her husband, Dan, had been waiting for her and was sitting on the navy blue couch facing the large picture window in their kitchen. He watched her slam the car door and tip toe over the slippery ice in the parking area behind the house. She didn't even bother to button her coat against the cold and let it flap around her in the wind. He knew her well enough to understand what her slumped shoulders meant. In the almost 25 years he had known her he had seen his wife that despondent just a few times before. He thought the worst.

When Annie walked into the kitchen she looked like a drowned cat. Her thick hair was soaked through, her stockings were sagging, and even her light tan leather briefcase had been darkened to a shade of mahogany by the pouring rain. Dan met her near the door and hugged her tight, helped her off with her coat, took her briefcase out of her hand, and led her back to the couch. Once she was settled, he stoked the burning wood in the nearby fire place and walked to the granite kitchen counter to warm up a cup of chamomile tea.  Overhead the reflection of the red and orange flames danced across the pewter pots and pans.

Annie had dropped onto the couch; her legs sprawled in front of her, her head supported by the comfortable sofa.  She kicked off her wet boots and waited for Dan.  He handed her the warm cup of tea then sat next to her and asked, "Well?" afraid to hear the answer.  While the news Annie relayed wasn't as bad as he expected, it wasn't good news either.  "I don't think James understands the seriousness of the burns," Annie continued.  "Give him time," Dan counseled.  "The whole situation is quite overwhelming for all of us.  It will sink in eventually." "Perhaps," was the only response Annie could muster.

Dan put his arm around his wife and pulled her close.  The ticking of the clock on the kitchen wall a few feet away grew louder in the silence, and in the quiet he found his thoughts wandering back to the first time he saw Annie.  She was leaning over a desk in a small office in the basement of Albany Law School, her brows drawn together in that expression that Dan knew too well, a woman on a mission.

She was a tiny little thing, maybe five feet tall.  At six feet he towered over her. She was a third-year law student at the time and he had graduated from Albany Law School two years before. Thanks to tons of money that had been handed down from one generation to the next in his family he did mostly pro bono work representing good people who couldn't afford to pay legal fees. He was also an assistant professor at the law school.

When Dan walked into the office, Annie stopped talking and the few other people in the room looked in his direction. "Hi, I'm Dan," he began, "I heard about your group and I'm here to help." Annie tried not to roll her eyes. She had heard about this guy, a rich white guy with an endless stream of money. She had heard he only worked pro bono cases and she was young enough to question his motives. She imagined all his good intentions would fade away real quick when he began to feel push-back for being a white guy defending black men in 1959.

To say she tolerated Dan's presence and participation as the group expanded might be a bit of an exaggeration, *barely* tolerated would be more exact. Most others in the group liked the guy. He was funny, a hard worker, and brilliant. As time went on everyone noticed how abrupt she was with Dan, sometimes cutting him off before he finished speaking but he never seemed annoyed. Then one night, after a meeting, he approached Annie and invited her out for coffee.

The invitation took her totally by surprise. "Where would you and I go for a cup of coffee?" she asked with more than a little sarcasm. "I know a few places," he responded pleasantly. "There's a great little twenty-four hour diner just down the road in Menands; the best ham and eggs in the area." "That's not what I meant," she threw back. "I know what you meant, Annie," he replied.

"It's not a problem." "Right, not a problem," she echoed. "I'm sorry," she continued, "I have to study for finals next week," and with that she turned on her heels and walked away.

Over the course of the next six months, Dan invited Annie out a number of times. Each time she declined. Even when he invited her to dinner to celebrate her graduation from law school, she said no. In the meantime, their small legal group was growing in reputation and thanks to a small grant from a local unnamed benefactor, Annie began to draw a modest salary to administer the group when she wasn't in court representing one of their clients. She only accepted the stipend when she was convinced the unnamed benefactor was not Dan or his family trust. Gradually she began to cut him some slack at meetings and although she hated to admit it, she had begun to rely on his expertise and had even come to respect his judgment. Around the same time, he seemed to have finally given up and stopped inviting her out and she noticed.

Then one warm spring night Annie was at the Madison Theater in Albany with a handful of friends from the office waiting to see Jerry Lewis in the "Absent-Minded Professor." She had lobbied for the group to see "Judgment at Nuremberg," but everyone else resisted, convincing her she needed to relax and laugh occasionally and they had heard the movie was hilarious. They were standing by the small refreshment counter when Dan walked into the lobby with the pretty blond first-year law student who was a new volunteer in their legal group. She was a friendly, bright young woman and Annie noticed shortly after she appeared in the office that she had her sights on Dan. Now there they were, Dan composed and smiling as he took all of the chiding from his friends. "Well, look who's here." "And look at who he is with." "Like older men, do ya?" "You can do better than Dan." The young blonde's cheeks turned a bright pink as a result of all of the attention and Annie couldn't help but notice that made her even more attractive. She also noticed when the blonde slipped her hand into Dan's arm.

Annie was angry, furious actually, and she knew it was stupid, that there was no reason for her to feel that way, but she couldn't help herself and couldn't stop herself from mumbling to her friends that she changed her mind, she was going home, as she stomped past Dan and out of the theater, cursing to herself as she marched down Madison Avenue toward her car.

"Annie" she heard him calling her, but she would not turn around. "Annie, wait a minute, are you okay?" She could hear his footsteps behind her but she would not turn around. "Okay dammit, have it your way," Dan yelled and his footsteps stopped. Annie continued walking hoping to hear his footsteps again, but she heard nothing but the passing cars. Then like an underwater diver surfacing after too long without air, she spun around and everything she had been holding in, everything she had never allowed herself to admit came rushing out in one long gasp.

"What? What do you want from me?" She yelled. "You know as well as I that nothing can come from this. Look at yourself, look at me. Are you foolish enough to believe that the color of our skin doesn't matter? Even if I did love you, which I'm not saying that I do, why begin something that has no future? Why start something that we both know will not end well. Your family would drop dead if you brought me home to meet them. Hell, my family would drop dead if I walked into their house with you." She stopped to take a breath.

Dan stood ten feet away, smiling. "How can you stand there and smile?" she demanded to know. "So," he began, "you think you'd like to meet my parents?" "You know you're an idiot," she responded, smiling now at the man with the foolish grin standing in front of her.

# 15

Caroline was glad to leave the hospital. She loved Grace, of course, but hated doctors and hospitals. She was buoyed by James' report after seeing Grace and had convinced herself, at least for the moment, that in a few weeks, a month tops, Grace would be healed and life would be back to normal. To celebrate, she took a few sips from the bottle of vodka she had left in her car. By the time she arrived home she had a nice buzz on and continued to drink until she passed out on the sofa. Then the dream returned.

It always started the same way, Jack and Caroline sitting across the kitchen table from his parents explaining their well thought out reasons why his parents should support their decision to get married in three months, the summer between Jack's third and fourth year at Dartmouth. They anticipated the "why not wait until after you graduate and have a solid job" logic and decided to counter that argument with the simple fact that they loved each other and wanted to be together. They would live on campus in married student housing, Caroline would find a job nearby and after graduation they would return to Troy where Jack would find an accounting job in a local business. He already had two offers from friends of his dad who had watched him grow up.

"Well, what about Caroline's age?" Kathryn asked her son. "She just turned 18 a few months ago and she's still a senior in high school for two more months. Is it really fair that she step into marriage before experiencing any of what the world has to offer?" Jack was ready for that one: "But, mom, you and dad got married when you were only 18 and dad was 21, exactly our ages." "I know," Kathryn replied, "but we had … well … an urgency." "I know, mom," Jack replied with a laugh. "I've always been good at math and when I was ten years old, I figured out that I was the "urgency."

"Oh," Kathryn replied with a jolt, "you're not …" "No, no," Jack replied. Caroline sat there fuming, she had always believed that Jack's parents thought he could find a girl better than her, that they didn't approve of her. Nevertheless, she was determined to marry Jack that summer no matter what his parents said. She wanted to elope but Jack felt compelled to get his parents' blessing.

On Saturday, July 18, 1964, at 11 a.m. Jack and Caroline were married at Sacred Heart Church, her childhood parish. In her dream she saw her handsome groom again, standing on the steps in front of the wooden altar, dressed in a new black suit, white shirt and black and gray striped tie. He didn't take his eyes off her as she walked down the aisle in a white lace tea length dress, a matching white lace pillbox balanced in front of the mound of blonde curls that her hair stylist had created just an hour before. White netting swooped down from the pillbox and covered her face. Monsignor Bourke, the parish pastor, stood in the center of the altar, waiting to perform the wedding ceremony, but Caroline couldn't help but wish it was Monsignor Martin, with his shock of white hair, waiting there instead. Monsignor Martin had befriended her when he was still Father Martin and the Pastor of Sacred Heart and she was a sad little third grader who just lost her parents, but he died unexpectedly less than a year before.

Jack's best man, his brother Frank, stood beside him and Caroline's best friend and maid of honor, Grace, waited on the altar dressed in a light pink chiffon shift. Caroline remembered thinking that Grace's smile was almost as big as Jack's. The colors and smells and people from the afternoon reception in Jack's parent's sprawling backyard flashed by in her dream.

The following year and a half was a magical time in their lives; they lived and breathed only for each other. Their tiny student housing apartment was more space than they needed. Jack's classes were not demanding and because they decided Caroline did not have to find a job, they had more time to be together than they had hoped.

Shortly after Jack's graduation they returned to Troy. Not long after they settled into their new apartment Jack was notified he had been drafted into the army. The battle was raging in Vietnam, but Jack and everyone else was convinced that due to his educational background he would find himself behind a desk in some office for the duration of his service. The night before Jack left for boot camp, their small apartment on Pawling Avenue, just up the street from Belden's Pond where they skated together as teenagers, was packed with family and friends wanting to shake Jack's hand and wish him well. Although they were glad to see everyone they could not wait for the last person to leave and spent the remaining hours before sunrise in each other's arms.

The next morning as they waited outside the recruitment office in downtown Troy for the bus that would take Jack away, Jack and his parents tried unsuccessfully to console an inconsolable Caroline. Jack half-jokingly quoted from his Order to Report for Induction, "Failure to report at the place and hour of the day named in this Order subjects the violator to imprisonment." Caroline didn't care, she preferred prison to combat. As the bus pulled away and traveled down Fourth Street, Jack leaned out the window and waved goodbye to the three most important people in his life.

As for Jack spending his military career behind a desk, that prediction turned out to be incorrect. To everyone's surprise, except for Jack's dad who took him hunting when he was a boy, it turned out that Jack was an expert marksman. He was assigned to an infantry firearm squad and flew from California to Vietnam within six months from the day he stepped on that bus.

Jack wrote to Caroline almost every day while he was in training at Fort Dix, New Jersey, but once he landed in Vietnam the letters dried up and months went by without a word or she received a handful of letters all on the same day. Her funny, optimistic Jack began to change before her eyes as his short notes and letters from Vietnam took on a sad and darker tone. Caroline found that she and Jack had switched roles. She wrote the letters filled with enthusiasm and encouragement, while his message was always the same; the only thing that mattered was coming home.

Caroline was taking clothes out of the washer in their apartment in the old Victorian on Pawling Avenue when she glanced out the second-story window and noticed the white station wagon with Red Cross painted on the side pull up to the curb in front of the house. She casually watched the somber man and woman walk up the sidewalk to the front of the building and wondered if they were soliciting donations. At the same time she tried to remember how much money she had in her wallet.

A few minutes later she heard a knock on the door. Otis Reddings' "Sitting on the Dock of the Bay" was playing on the kitchen radio and she continued singing along as she made her way to the door. She wasn't surprised to see the couple from the Red Cross standing there. "Wait just a minute and I'll see what I have in my wallet," she said as she began to walk away. "Mam," the man began, "are you Mrs. John Gardinier, Army Sergeant John Gardinier's wife?" Caroline responded with a smile, "Yes, yes, I am." After a moment the man continued, "We are sorry to inform you mam, that your husband, Sergeant John Gardinier was killed in the line of duty on

March 14$^{th}$ in Vietnam." He continued, "Within the next week, his remains will be flown from South Vietnam to Dover Air Force Base in Delaware for final processing."

Caroline had stopped listening after the man's first sentence. "No, no, there must be a mistake," she whispered. "Jack is not dead. I know he isn't; if he were, I would know it, I would feel it." The couple stepped into the small parlor and closed the door. "You said March 14, that was weeks ago, and I have a letter that just arrived yesterday from Jack." Caroline spun around and walked to the small desk in the corner where she began rummaging through a pile of papers as though finding the letter would prove somehow that Jack was still alive.

The woman tried to comfort Caroline and reached for her, but Caroline pulled away. Louder now, "No, no, that's impossible; I just received a letter from Jack," Caroline turned her back again and continued looking through the envelopes stacked neatly on the desk, this time with a new urgency. "I know this is difficult, "the woman began. Caroline spun around, screaming now, "No, no, you don't know, you know nothing. Get out of my house!" The man spoke, "Mam, we can't leave you like this, is there someone you can call?" "It's none of your business," Caroline screamed back while grabbing their arms and trying to physically force them across the floor and out the door. "Get the fuck out of my house," she yelled, pushing them forward until she looked up and saw Kathryn standing in the doorway, her face as white as a glove.

"Kathryn," Caroline pleaded, "they're trying to tell me that Jack is dead, but he can't be, I just got a letter." Kathryn grasped the scene in front of her immediately, her boy was gone, and while she had always been the strong one, on that morning Kathryn crumpled into a ball and fell to the floor.

In Caroline's dreams the events of the following weeks flash by in colors of red, white, and blue and visions of young men with sad faces dressed in military uniforms walking in cadence beside the box that carried her Jack. Even the sweet smell of the flowers made her sick to her stomach. The dream always ended the same way: she and Grace sitting next to each other at St. Joseph's Cemetery near the Griswold Heights Apartments, practically across the street from the building where she lived with her aunt as a child. A folded flag handed to her and rifle shots, each shot echoing through the still cemetery and piercing her heart. Caroline aching to take off her shoes and run away, run across the manicured dewy green lawns until she disappeared, but Grace holding her hand as if Caroline was a fragile balloon that would float away if she let go.

That's where the dream always ended and that's when Caroline always woke up in disbelief.

# 16

The night of the day Grace was burned Kathryn kept thinking about her shop and how she never would have opened it if it weren't for Grace's encouragement. Both of her boys were out of college and had started lives of their own, Frank married with a child on the way and Timothy enjoying the single life in Boston. Her husband John's hardware store was booming. During the years since Jack's death John lost himself in his business a little more each year and every year the business became more successful.

Kathryn understood and knew it was John's way of dealing with the loss. The patterns of John's grief were obvious to anyone who knew him. As the anniversary of Jack's death approached, John's moods became darker and she and her sons gave him a wide berth until, like a bear from hibernation, he woke up one morning and suddenly life was lighter. Her sons had formed the habit of calling her the week before the anniversary to be sure she had the support she needed during that time because they knew their dad went into a place where no one, not even Kathryn, could follow.

One morning about six years after Jack's death, Grace

and Kathryn were sitting in Grace's kitchen and Kathryn was venting about having nothing to do now that the boys were out on their own and John was so involved in the store. Grace casually remarked that she should open a knitting shop. A light bulb went on in Kathryn's head and she was off.

Kathryn and Grace spent months looking for the right location, and Caroline often joined them except for the days when she wasn't "feeling well." They bounced every location possibility off of Hedy and Annie whose jobs kept them too busy to join the search, and like dedicated gardeners planning a spring flower garden, they poured over catalogue after catalogue of different types and colors of yarn until Kathryn's formal dining room at home began to look like a yarn warehouse.

Then one day a friend of John's told him about a small empty storefront located on Third Street in downtown Troy. At first Kathryn disregarded the space because it was clear to anyone raised in Troy that downtown was slowly being abandoned for the shopping malls that had sprung up in nearby communities. Nevertheless, one Saturday morning Kathryn, Hedy, Grace, Caroline, and Annie met in front of the storefront and it was love at first sight.

Like so many of the buildings in downtown Troy, the little space was a Victorian gem. The original etched glass on the front door was reinforced with black wrought iron bars made in the Burden Iron Works at the turn of the 20th Century. Kathryn passed by the remains of the

Burden Iron Works each day on the way to work and often daydreamed about what Troy looked like back then.

Inside, the original glass and wood display case extended ten feet on the left, and to Kathryn's surprise, there was a huge black functioning antique cash register on the countertop. On the right a large open space with wide paneled wood floors met matching wood paneled walls that rose 15 feet high until they touched a white tin ceiling with hand engraved detailing. If it weren't for the nine foot wide, five foot high bay window facing Third Street, the room would have been in darkness even on that sunny Saturday morning, but the light streaming in the big window lit up the entire shop.

And as if all of that wasn't enough, there were 40 built-in cubby holes on the back wall of the main room just waiting to be filled with skeins of yarn. A small office space not larger than 6' by 6' and an even smaller half bath were tucked in the back. Kathryn took a quick look around and knew she had found her shop.

Although it seemed counterintuitive to open her yarn shop in a city where businesses were evaporating, she reminded her friends that at least there would be plenty of parking spaces available on the street and, since all of her current customers were accustomed to coming to her home for lessons, she imagined no one would mind a shift in the location. Besides, the plans she had for the space would make it much more comfortable than her kitchen table.

Over the next two months Kathryn threw herself into

preparing her new shop. Her friends helped when they had the time and having a husband who was a handyman and owned a hardware store certainly helped with the minor repairs to the plumbing and woodwork. John even added a dozen more cubby holes to the back wall to accommodate all of the yarn Kathryn had ordered.

Sooner than she could imagine, it was the day of the open house. All of her customers, friends and family had been invited to visit the shop that chilly Sunday afternoon in early November. The gray day was a perfect backdrop for the sight that greeted them when they opened the shop's front door and stepped inside. A warm and golden light from a small antique crystal chandelier hanging over the polished counter and cash register welcomed each visitor until their eyes were drawn to the skeins of yarn bursting from the cubbies on the back wall. The entire wall was an explosion of color and, like Monet's flower gardens at his home in Giverny, the yarn flowed from one color to the next like a painter's palette until the entire color spectrum appeared before their eyes; small batches of color blends breaking the spectrum here and there. As each person entered the shop for the first time, the reaction was the same, a gasp followed by a wow.

Two matching red plaid overstuffed sofas faced each other in front of the window; a six-foot long pine coffee table that John made as a surprise open house gift for Kathryn separated the two couches. At the end of each couch, matching pine coffee tables held white, red, and dark blue ceramic lamps with oriental landscapes and large red cotton lamp shades that focused the light down onto the tabletops. Huge red and white throw pillows in random designs were scattered about, most occupied on the afternoon of the open house. Five terra cotta planters, each filled with red geraniums, spanned the width of the long bay windowsill, Kathryn's private homage to her circle of friends. Overall the effect was very pleasing, cozy, and welcoming.

The smell of hot mulled apple cider, fresh baked Toll House chocolate chip cookies (Grace's, of course), assorted hors d'oeuvres, and the faint scent of patchouli filled the air while cigarette smoke hung over the crowd like a cloud.

All afternoon Kathryn watched Caroline balance herself on the arm of one of the couches and noticed her position became more precarious every time she returned from the makeshift wine bar John had set up in the corner. Since Jack's death, Kathryn had become Caroline's touchstone. Every time Caroline bottomed out, every time she left rehab, (twice since Jack), every time a relationship or marriage fell apart, (three times since Jack,) -- although to be fair the last marriage ended when Caroline became a widow -- Kathryn and John were there to support her. They had grown to love and truly care for her and taking care of Caroline was the very least they could do for their Jack.

The front door opened and closed all afternoon with visitors coming and going. In her mind's eye, Kathryn saw Grace and James rush in, late as usual, Grace filled to the brim with her unborn twin daughters.

# 17

Grace opened her eyes, unsure of where she was. She knew she was lying down. There was something over her chest that blocked her view. The overhead lights were too bright, shining in her eyes. She tried to lift her arm to block the glare, but couldn't seem to move it although it didn't feel constrained. She wondered who the people were walking around the room, but didn't feel threatened by them. Their whispers were mumbles in her ears. She tried to speak, to say hello, but they ignored her or didn't hear her, she wasn't sure which.

She felt fine lying there and had no desire to move. She noticed the pleasant man she had seen before was sitting on a chair next to her. He was speaking to her, but she couldn't make out what he was saying. This was not the first time she woke and found herself in the bright room, saw the pleasant man and the activity around her, but then something always happened and it all went to black before anyone knew she was awake.

She relaxed in the bright room for a while before it began. A soft ripple of discomfort that kept repeating until it grew into overwhelming and continuous waves of pain that crashed down upon her and took her breath away.

She could feel her heart pounding in her chest and heard the rhythm of her rapid heartbeat echoing in the room. Then there was activity around her and merciful sleep.

# 18

Hedy couldn't sleep. The anxiety that came with concern for Grace did not come alone. Every irrational fear that she was able to minimize under normal circumstances stormed the gate and invaded her thoughts. Fear for Grace's well-being had opened the flood waters and Hedy found herself carried away, overwhelmed by anxiety. After an hour of tossing and turning in bed she unraveled herself from the twisted sheets and shuffled through the quiet house toward the kitchen hoping that a cup of chamomile tea would calm her.

Five minutes later, a warm mug of tea in her hand, she walked to her study off the front hall. In the dark she maneuvered her way around the few pieces of furniture in the room and switched on the lamp on the desktop. The whimsical lamp had been a birthday gift from her to Christopher; a dapper dark green metal frog dressed in a fitted Edwardian suit, a scarf tied casually around his neck, sat on a metal water lily under a square black lamp shade. Every time she turned it on, she remembered how much he loved that silly lamp. Smiling, she sat down in Christopher's well-worn leather swivel chair that she could not bring herself to throw away and in her mind's eye could still see him lounging in that chair in their California apartment, his long legs crossed at the knees and a brown leather slipper dangling precariously from his right foot.

Then another, less pleasant, memory; Christopher sitting at the desk reviewing blueprints in their California apartment, sitting in the very chair she sat in now, when suddenly his chair began to slowly roll backwards. Sitting just a few feet away, Hedy looked up from the book she was reading and saw Christopher with his head resting on the desk and the chair rolling out from underneath him. At first she thought he was joking, until he didn't respond to her laughter. A brain aneurism took him suddenly and completely.

With Christopher gone, she had no reason to stay in California so she packed just a few things that were important to her and returned to Troy a 40-year old widow. When she got off the plane that day the only person she expected to meet was the undertaker who would collect Christopher's remains and prepare for his services. She had told her ailing parents to stay home, that she would take a taxi.

She still remembered the surprise and relief she felt when she saw John Gardiner, Christopher's lifelong friend, and his wife, Kathryn, talking with the undertaker. John and Kathryn were by her side every moment during the horrible week that followed and Hedy still considered them her dearest friends.

Absentmindedly, Hedy picked up the day-old newspaper lying on the desk. Ayatollah Khomeini was still holding the US hostages and had decided that Iran's parliament would decide their fate. The band AC/DC's lead singer, Bon Scott, drank himself to death in London. Christopher would hate that news she thought, his copy of their album Highway to Hell was still on the bookshelf behind her. President Carter announced the U.S. would boycott the Summer Olympic Games in Moscow. The only good piece of news was the U.S. hockey team's win over Russia at the Winter Olympics in Lake Placid a few days before.

She stood up and dropped the paper on the desk. Even though it was only 4 a.m., she decided to dress and go to the hospital thinking that if he were still there, James might need a break. After a quick shower she slipped into a pair of black slacks, a soft white angora V-neck sweater, and pulled on a pair of black ankle boots that she found on the boot tray near the front door.

The hospital was quiet when she arrived an hour later. A solitary nurse sat behind the desk at the nurses' station. Hedy asked how Grace was doing and, as expected, there was no real change, she was holding her own. The waiting room was empty; James had not arrived yet, so she turned to select the most comfortable chair in a waiting room of sad choices. As she sat down the door to the Burn Unit swung open and Grace's doctors walked out, their brows furrowed and deep in conversation. She watched them walk to the duty nurse where they began a conversation Hedy did not understand. Eventually they handed their notes to the nurse and Dr. Watson walked down the hallway toward the elevator; Dr. Devan turned to walk back into the Burn Unit, saw Hedy sitting there, smiled and walked over to her.

"What are you doing here so early?" he wanted to know. "Oh, I couldn't sleep" Hedy said a bit sheepishly, "and wanted to give James a break if he was here. It must be so difficult for him with the kids asking questions." "I know, it's a horrible situation," Dr. Devan agreed candidly. "I see these scalding accidents much more often than I would like."

"You know I can't tell you anything specific, Hedy" he began as he sat down in the chair across from her, surprising her that he remembered her name, "but, things are not any worse," he added encouragingly. From somewhere deep inside her the question slipped out, "Is she going to die, doctor?" He looked away and exhaled while his shoulders dropped. "Grace is doing as well as we can expect under the circumstances, Hedy," he replied. "All her vitals are holding their own."

'How is Grace, today?" James asked crossing the room with a few long strides. Dr. Devan smiled weakly at Hedy, then stood up, shook hands with James, and pointed him down the hallway saying, "Walk with me."

It seemed to Hedy that hours went by before James returned. She tried to read his facial expression as he walked toward her. "Just as they thought," James began as he sat down beside her. "First, second and third degree burns. It will be days before they know for sure how well Grace will do. Right now her system is under tremendous pressure. She's having trouble breathing occasionally and they're not sure if her lungs are struggling, or if the sudden onset of pain is causing her to hold her breath, challenging her lungs. They're walking a delicate line trying to keep her comfortable with the minimum amount of pain killers. She'll be on pain killers for quite a while and because they can be so addictive, the doctors have to be careful of the dosage." He took a breath, and then continued, "It looks like Grace's right knee has a fourth degree burn, and there is some muscle damage and maybe bone damage too. It will have to be monitored carefully to avoid infection. If infection takes hold, in the worst case scenario ... never mind, we won't get to that point," James finished confidently.

Hedy squeezed James' hand waiting for more information but he fell silent. "Can I get you a cup of coffee?" she asked when it was clear he had nothing more to add. "No, thanks," he replied. "I've had so much coffee during the last 24 hours that my eyelids won't close. The doctor told me I can sit with Grace this morning after the nurses are finished cleaning her wounds so I'm going to plant myself here for a few minutes and take a breath." "Sure," Hedy replied, and then stood up. "I'm going to the cafeteria and get a cup of tea."

Hedy was a few feet away when James said, "Hedy, by the way, Dr. Devan mentioned you, what a pleasant woman you are, and he wondered out loud if you are married or seeing anyone." Hedy turned around with a quizzical look on her face. "You're kidding, right?" she asked. "No, I'm not," James replied. "I told him you had a number of male admirers, but not one man in particular. I think he likes you." "Oh, please," Hedy replied, "you made me sound like a hussy." For the first time in days, a smile flashed across James' face before he turned his attention back to the glass door of the Burn Unit.

In spite of everything that was happening, an unexpected and, in Hedy's opinion, inappropriate smile washed across her face as she rode the elevator down to the basement cafeteria.

# 19

Caroline crawled out of bed and headed for the vodka in the freezer. She promised herself tomorrow, tomorrow, she would stop drinking. Tomorrow she would be strong for Grace but tonight, well, the dream had returned and vodka made her forget. Grace would understand.

Two hours later the sun was beginning to break the horizon and Caroline sat at her ridiculously long dining room table on one of twelve white satin brocade dining room chairs. She was too drunk to stand. Out of the corner of her eye she saw the small writing table within arm's reach and without much thought, stretched over while barely balancing herself on the chair, and managed to grab the red box of writing paper and a pen. With exaggerated care she opened the box and then with trembling fingers struggled to pull out one sheet of the fine white paper. After a considerable amount of time, she finally laid the sheet of paper on the dining room table where half of the expensive sheet of stationery settled into a pool of water created by a stray and melting ice cube. Cursing, she picked up the wet sheet, shook it and made what to her seemed like a reasonable decision, to write only on the dry section.

There was something she had wanted to tell Grace for years, and her alcohol-addled mind decided now was the perfect time. After all, Grace would understand, Grace always understood. Caroline thought it would clear the air, make everything new again and, while Grace had no idea the air needed to be cleared, Caroline needed to confess.

Caroline poured a fresh glass of vodka and began to write. Fifteen minutes later the letter was written, signed, and shoved into a matching white envelope with Caroline's monogram embossed in gold across the back flap. With a sense of relief that only a long overdue confession can produce, she put her head down on the table and fell into a deep sleep.

Two hours later Kathryn was on her way to the Medical Center to check on Grace and relieve James if necessary when, on a whim, she took a sudden left turn and drove the ten minutes out of her way to Caroline's house. Everyone knew, and no one knew better than Kathryn, how fragile Caroline was and she was afraid if anything happened to Grace, Caroline would simply not survive.

When Caroline and her late husband, Tom, first moved into that huge monster of a house, they gave Kathryn a key. On this morning, like most, she didn't need to use it because once again Caroline had forgotten to lock the front door. Making her way through the large foyer, Kathryn listened for signs of life and/or snoring sounds. She didn't actually expect to find Caroline up and about at 8:30 in the morning. She did expect to find her sprawled across the bed, not draped across the dining room table. That's new, Kathryn thought, I haven't seen that one before.

After a quick evaluation, she decided Caroline was safe where she was, that she was not in danger of falling off the chair. Sighing, Kathryn walked past Caroline into the parlor where she checked to be sure the thermostat was set correctly, then did a quick sweep of the house to be sure everything was turned off.

As she passed back through the dining room on her way to the front door, Kathryn saw the envelope on the table with Grace's name scrawled across the front. I'll be damned, she thought, at least Caroline had the presence of mind to write her friend a get-well note. Picking up the envelope Kathryn tucked it into the pocket of her winter coat for safe keeping, thinking James might be looking for something to read to Grace as he sat by her bedside.

Locking the door behind her, Kathryn climbed into her old station wagon, cranked up the heat and pointed it toward Albany Medical Center.

The sound of the old wagon pulling out of the gravel driveway disturbed Caroline's sleep. She peered at the world through squinting eyes set in a throbbing head, then stood up and stumbled her way to the bathroom. After throwing cold water on her face, she began to get a creeping sense that she had done something terrible, her stomach tightened when it dawned on her what was wrong. No, she thought, I didn't write that letter; tell me I didn't write that letter. Now her thoughts were becoming frantic. She rushed to the dining room and shuffled through the clutter but found no letter. Thank goodness, she thought. Feeling an overwhelming since of relief, Caroline walked to the bedroom, changed into cotton pjs and fell into a deep sleep.

Even after all of the years of foolish behavior, bad judgment, health scares that Kathryn had lived through with Caroline, she would still be stunned by the content of the letter she carried in her coat pocket. The words would be unimaginable to her, perhaps even unforgiveable.

# 20

Annie was notorious for canceling personal appointments. She considered canceling her OB/GYN appointment the day following Grace's accident but had already canceled the same appointment twice and consequently feared the wrath of Dr. Thomas. She also had a few symptoms that she assumed were related to the early onset of menopause and thought Dr. Thomas might be able to prescribe something that would return the zip to her 44-year old steps.

Before leaving home she dialed the hospital and was assured by the floor nurse that there was no significant change in Grace's condition. Deciding to take that as good news, Annie left for her doctor's office on Second Street in Troy near Washington Park. It was always difficult finding a parking spot near the office and she knew it would be even more difficult that day because of the recent snowstorm.

Driving down Second Street there were plenty of parking spaces that had been cleared of snow but the plastic lawn chairs set in each of the spaces were a clear warning to any intrepid driver that the person or persons who spent hours shoveling and clearing snow from those spaces would not tolerate interlopers. Annie even had a case once where she defended a client involved in a fistfight with a man who had the audacity to remove one of those chairs and slide into a cleared parking space. She smiled remembering how the judge, a Troy boy born and raised, found her client not guilty of assault because everyone knew removing a lawn chair under those circumstances was a clear provocation.

She found an unclaimed parking spot four blocks from the doctor's office and considered herself lucky. It was a cold morning. An hour ago the thermometer outside her kitchen window read 10 degrees, but the sun was shining, the sky was blue, and the wind was calm. She enjoyed the walk past St. Mary's Church and the old row houses surrounding Washington Park, row houses once occupied by the families of the pillars of Troy's industrial past. The park itself filled a city block and was enclosed by an old black Troy built wrought iron fence. She could imagine those streets in their hay day, cobblestoned and filled with the sounds of busy merchants in horse drawn carts delivering coal, groceries, and ice, pulling their carts into the alleys behind the houses and waiting for housekeepers in stark black dresses, with long hair twisted into severe braids wrapped around the crown of their heads to count out the payment and send them on their way.

The office was filled with patients when Annie arrived. She checked in at the reception area and found an unoccupied chair. A half hour later she was escorted to an examining room where eventually Dr. Thomas opened the door and walked in while flipping through Annie's medical folder. Annie accepted the doctor's ribbing about her canceled appointments good naturedly. Everything was progressing routinely during the examination until Annie heard the doctor whisper "What's this?" and that got Annie's attention. "What?" Annie asked. "Just give me a few minutes, I want to check something out," Dr. Thomas responded. "I'll be right back." "Should I be concerned?" Annie asked the doctor's back. "Just relax, I'll be right back" was the response.

After what seemed like hours but was actually a few minutes, Dr. Thomas returned with a nurse who was rolling a large white machine in front of her. "Now lay back and relax," the doctor told Annie. Once Annie was settled the doctor separated the blue paper vest Annie was wearing. "This is going to be cold," she warned before squeezing a clear cream from a tube and spreading it on Annie's stomach. When the nurse finished plugging in the machine, Dr. Thomas began to carefully move a metal bar over Annie's middle. "What are you looking for?" Annie asked her voice getting higher. "I'll tell you in a minute," the doctor replied, then "there you are."

"What are you talking about?" Annie blurted, "there who is?" The reality of the moment had not quite caught up with her yet. Smiling, the doctor rolled the machine toward Annie so that she could see the screen. At first she didn't understand what she was seeing. There was some movement on a black and white screen. Suddenly the outline jumped out at her. "That's not ..." she began. "Oh, yes, it is." Dr. Thomas replied with a grin on her face. "It can't be," Annie responded, "we've been told a thousand times that we would never have a child of our own. YOU told me that yourself more than once," she ended.

"Evidently there was a change, something shifted," Carol Thomas replied, the silly grin still on her face. "I'm 44 years old, I can't have a child at this age, "Annie stated. "It looks to me like you can," the doctor replied, then more seriously, "I'll do a few tests to be sure, but it looks like a healthy three month old fetus." "Three-month old!!" Annie screamed. "Calm down," the doctor said as she patted Annie's arm. "I'll do some tests and then we'll talk. In the meantime, take your time getting dressed and I'll see you in my office." Then, turning to the nurse, "draw blood and ..." Annie stopped listening.

A half hour later Annie was fully dressed and sitting in the doctor's small office staring at a break-apart plastic model of a woman's uterus accommodating a growing fetus at different stages. She thought she was fully dressed, she couldn't keep the same thought in her head for more than a second since she saw the ultrasound.

Dr. Thomas did her best not to smile when she entered the office carrying Annie's file. "As far as I can tell, Annie, you are definitely pregnant and based on measurements, you're probably around 2 ½ to 3 months along." She stopped to let that sink in. "I know this is a shock, Annie, and that you have a lot to think about. Go home, put your feet up and talk with Dan. I know he's going to be thrilled." "Well, sure," Annie commented thinking out loud, "he's not the one whose 44-year old body is going to have to go through this." The doctor continued, "Everything looks normal, Annie. We can schedule an amniocentesis test to see if the baby is well. The test will also tell us the sex of your child. A needle is gently inserted into your belly and into your uterus, amniotic fluid is withdrawn and tested for any defects. I recommend the test for all of my older patients. I can see by the tests we've done today that it will be a few more weeks before your body is ready for the amniocentesis."

"I want you to understand that I am here for you. If anything happens that concerns you pick up the phone. If it's after office hours the exchange will get in touch with me." Reaching across the desk she handed Annie a prescription, "have this filled right away, they're prenatal vitamins. Call me Monday, I'll be here and we'll talk some more about what's happening. For now, go home and tell Dan the good news."

Annie took the prescription, gave her doctor a weak smile, and dream walked out of the office, down the concrete steps and the four blocks back to her car. I didn't see this one coming, she thought as she turned the ignition key while wondering if she should turn up the heat for the baby. See, she thought, you've got me taking care of you already.

# 21

Driving home Annie's thoughts kept slipping back to the early days of her relationship with Dan.

She had always been amazed by Dan's lack of concern about the opinions of others. He understood her reluctance to date openly, a black woman and white man would not be well received by all in the early 1960s, even in Albany, New York, but he didn't care. When they became engaged, he bought her the biggest diamond solitaire engagement ring she had ever seen. It was so huge she was embarrassed to wear it at her pro bono appointments and it took years of consistent conversations before Dan finally convinced her that she didn't have to be ashamed of being wealthy.

While Dan began planning a huge traditional church wedding, Annie was still struggling with how to tell her parents they were engaged. She knew they liked Dan, maybe even loved him, but she also knew they disapproved of their relationship. Mostly they were afraid for Annie, the criticism they feared she would face as a white man's wife. They had no idea how wealthy Dan was, and that up to a certain point that wealth could insulate them from the bigots in the world.

Dan's parents were as open and welcoming to Annie as Dan had always been. They didn't even blink the first time Dan brought her to their home. Yet, before their wedding, Dan's dad sat down with him one evening after dinner and discussed all the potential issues they could face during their married life. Dan thanked him for his concern but assured him they were committed enough to face every challenge. Dan was a brilliant man and had no delusions about what the future could bring, but he wanted what he wanted and that was Annie.

In the end, Annie and Dan were married on a rainy, late Saturday morning in June in the Church of St. Charles Borromeo on West 141st Street in Harlem, NY, the church where Annie grew up. One hundred of their closest friends and family members attended the service followed by a small elegant afternoon reception in the Terrace Room at the Plaza Hotel. Nelson Rockefeller, who was Governor of New York at the time, and his wife Happy, both personal friends of Dan's parents, attended both events.

Annie wore a white lace ballet length wedding gown and a shoulder length veil held in place by a modest rhinestone headband. She and her mom spent months walking around New York City looking for "the" dress only to realize two months before the wedding that Carla, a retired seamstress and life-long friend and neighbor was the answer to their problem of finding a dress to fit Annie's tiny frame. Carla was delighted to come out of retirement for the occasion and the dress she created was magnificent.

Annie's cousin Fran's three-year old daughter, Sally, was an adorable flower girl in her lavender lace dress and matching ballet slippers. Dan's almost three-year old nephew, Mike, stole the show when he marched down the aisle wearing a tiny tux and tails hugging his teddy bear to his chest. Annie chose her closest friend and cousin, Donna, as her maid of honor, and Dan's sister, Marie, as her matron of honor. They both wore the palest shade of lavender while the other four bridesmaids wore a deeper hue.

Since Dan could not make a decision, his brothers Jim and Joe were his best men. Friends from college and law school were his groomsmen and all looked dashing in their black tails and gray vests.

No one but Dan knew where they were going on their honeymoon. After saying their good-byes at the reception, they took a taxi to LaGuardia Airport and in four hours were checking into a very posh hotel room in Montego Bay, Jamaica. It was a trip to remember and since then they had lived a mostly charmed life. The only thing missing were the children they were told they would never have.

Pulling into the parking area behind her house, Annie was surprised when she realized she had arrived there safe and sound; her mind had been so preoccupied it seemed the car had found its way home without her.

# 22

Beyond the door to the Burn Unit, Grace was flustered and confused. She was aware of activity around her and the sound of muffled voices, two men in serious conversation. She could feel a sensation on her chest and thighs, as though a hundred band aids were being pulled off all at once. She tried to ask what was happening, indeed thought she had, but the words she heard remained muffled and unclear. Someone was lifting her right leg and gently bending it at the knee. A cold metal machine rolled close, the voices disappeared, and then returned.

Grace wondered where the kind man was in this crowd, the man that read to her in a soothing voice, and kissed her forehead when he went away. Then she felt it and panicked. It always started unexpectedly, an annoyance at first that she was sure she could eliminate if she was only able to move, to adjust the way she was laying. Within seconds the monster roared in changing any light to dark, smothering her, taking her breath away, a pain unlike anything she had ever felt. She screamed, raged against it because she had no choice, but her resistance was futile, thousands of red hot spikes stabbed at her and then sleep came and the monster receded, driven back into its lair by modern medicine.

# 23

James dozed off in the waiting room and jumped when the nurse touched his shoulder, finally giving him the okay to sit with Gracie for a while. After helping him slip into the blue protective clothing and sliding the white mask over his mouth, the nurse led James into the area where Grace's hospital bed was located. As they approached, she slid a faux leather maroon recliner next to the bed for James and reminded him not to take Grace's hand or touch her in any way. She left him with strict orders to call her if Grace regained consciousness.

As he sank into the sagging maroon chair, James felt as though he had stepped into an alternate universe; a universe where beeping machines mimicked the human heartbeat; where multiple tubes drooped down from plastic bags filled with unknown liquids and disappeared under the white blanket that covered his Grace. A universe lit by gigantic overhead lamps that shone brighter than any sun he had ever seen. Even his protective clothing was surreal, right down to the blue matching paper hat and slippers.

He remembered the first time he saw Grace at Belden's Pond. Jack had begged him to skate with this unknown young girl so that he could skate with Caroline. James felt put upon being asked to skate with a girl still in grammar school, but he was taking one for the team as he skated slowly toward Grace. As soon as she turned around to face him, everything changed. She was beautiful standing there in the frigid night air, her face shining, her cheeks red, and her innocent and trusting eyes looking back at him. He attempted conversation, but she seemed so uninterested that when the skate was finished he never had the nerve to approach her again until one night years later when they were both at a small house warming party at Jack's apartment after he and Caroline returned from Dartmouth.

No longer the awkward school boy, James approached Grace and reminded her about their first meeting at Belden's Pond. Grace was shocked to learn he was that boy and they laughed at the memory, then talked about their mutual friends, Jack and Caroline, and finally exchanged stories about their experiences in the neighborhood where they grew up.

Grace was beginning her third year at Russell Sage College in Troy, working toward her teaching degree. James had graduated from Siena College in the spring and was teaching at LaSalle Institute, his and Jack's high school alma mater. Their mutual interest in teaching drew them together.

They were married three years later on a sunny January morning at the same church where Caroline and Jack were married almost five years before. James could still see Grace walking down the aisle, the warm jeweled colors of the stained glass windows reflecting off her long white A-line gown, her hands tucked inside a white fur muff covered with white and pink roses. When she met him at the altar, the white fur trim at the collar of her dress surrounded her face like a halo and took his breath away.

Their two best friends, Jack and Caroline, were missing that day; Jack gone almost two years and Caroline in rehab for the first time. James knew Grace always suspected that their pending wedding brought back more memories of Jack than Caroline could handle, so she literally drowned her sadness in vodka during the months leading up to their wedding.

Lost in his memories, without even thinking about it, James reached over to pick up Grace's pink hand resting on the pristine white sheet tucked into the hospital bed, but stopped short of touching it when the nurse's cautionary words resounded in his ears. He was surprised to see that Grace's hand looked perfectly normal, the light pink skin smooth, unchanged.

Although he tried to be strong, he knew in his heart that he was weak and even though she never said it he was sure Gracie knew it too. She had her reasons for accepting him, faults and all, for overlooking his weaknesses, and on those few occasions when he was totally honest with himself, he suspected her kindness had more to do with their children than with him. Now here they were, the strong one fallen, the weakest left to carry on.

Whenever their girls injured themselves, cut a finger, broke a bone, James stepped back and Grace handled medical emergencies. A blown fuse leaving the house in darkness, a furnace that stopped working in the dead of winter, a water pipe exploding in the basement or under the kitchen sink, those emergencies James could handle, but physical injuries were beyond him.

Nevertheless, for Grace he would be strong. He sat in that room listening to the humming and buzzing while the smell of antiseptic mingling with the "hospital smell" that he hated assaulted his nose. He forced his eyes to look at his beautiful Grace lying helplessly, knowing that her delicate white skin was seriously damaged, perhaps beyond repair.

Suddenly his eyes noticed a bright red rim on her arm at the junction where her forearm met the bandages. Knowing he shouldn't, he reached over and watched as his hand lifted the bandages revealing what looked like raw meat where the pink flesh of her upper arm should be. It took a few seconds for the shock of what he was seeing to register and when it did he recoiled backwards, the force of his body knocking the maroon recliner on its back. Two nurses rushed toward him, Grace began to moan, and tears rushed down his face.

One nurse quickly ushered him out of the area while the other began monitoring the equipment that surrounded Grace. "What happened?," the nurse asked James. He tried to answer but was sobbing and couldn't get the words out. "Here, sit down," the nurse said as she steered him toward the nearest chair. "I never imagined it would be so bad," James squeaked out as his watery eyes stared at the nurse. "Her skin is gone, her arm looks like ..." and his voice trailed off. "How did you see her injuries?" the nurse asked. Looking and sounding like a six-year old boy, he blurted out what he had done.

Taking a deep breath, the nurse sat down next to him. "Your wife is burned over 55% of her body. As you know, a number of skin grafts have been completed so far and one minor procedure to release the tightness caused by skin repairing itself around her left shoulder. As the doctors have told you, she has a 4$^{th}$ degree burn on her left knee that has affected her kneecap. The therapy treatments on her knee are showing signs of possible progress, but one infection can reverse the progress she has made. One infection could change her situation to one of life and death. You need to understand how important this is and you cannot let your idle curiosity get the better of you. You cannot touch her or her bandages," the nurse spoke strongly, but not without pity in her voice.

"Now," she finished, "sit here until you've pulled yourself together and then go home. Come back tomorrow. If there's a change, we will contact you." After gently patting his shoulder, the nurse joined her colleague at Grace's bedside.

# 24

Grace screamed and her eyes snapped open in alarm. At least she thought she screamed, but no one seemed to notice. The pleasant man was backing away from her, tripping over a chair that was toppled on the floor. She could feel her heart pounding in her chest.

What happened to James, she asked herself. James? And just like that she knew he was her husband. Suddenly her thoughts were flooded with images and conversations. Children, she thought, we have children. Where are they? Where am I? WHO am I?

He looks so frightened. Of me? Why is he backing away? Where am I? What's happened? Am I dead? Am I dying? What's happening?

They were her last frantic thoughts before the sedative kicked in.

# 25

As soon as she was inside the house Annie headed for the stairs and walked straight to her bedroom. She tossed her overcoat onto the bed and, turning sideways, studied her silhouette in the tall mirror. She saw nothing to indicate she was three months pregnant. There was a barely noticeable bump below her waist, a bump she had chalked up to middle-age spread. Well, that's some middle-age spread, she joked to herself.

Sitting on the edge of the bed, she pulled the sonogram image from the pocket of her coat and looked at the outline of her child. "My child" she said out loud. Wasn't it just like life to give you what you wanted most after you had given up and moved on? Dr. Thomas had given Annie the image of the baby even though sonograms and ultrasounds were a relatively new medical advancement at that time and only used if there was a troubled pregnancy. Dr. Thomas told Annie she was giving her the sonogram image because Annie was so incredulous about the pregnancy that the doctor felt Annie needed documented proof.

Dropping her body back onto the bed, Annie closed her eyes and began to imagine what her daughter would look like. Daughter? She laughed, why daughter, she wondered? Then her mind drifted to frilly dresses and baseball uniforms while her body drifted off to sleep.

The sound of Dan stomping his snow covered boots on the throw rug by the kitchen door woke her. The bedside clock told her it was 4:30 and the sliver of daylight giving way to the night sky outside her bedroom window told her it was the afternoon. At the speed of light her thoughts flashed to why she was sleeping in the middle of the afternoon, then to the sonogram still resting on her stomach. Not sure why, she stuck the little piece of film back into her coat pocket then hung the coat in the closet. She yelled down to Dan, telling him she was home.

"What are you doing home so early?," he yelled back up the stairs. "I was tired and my afternoon appointments were canceled," she lied, "so I thought I'd come home and take a nap." "Are you feeling okay?," Dan asked as he climbed the stairs. "Sure, I'm fine," she said.

Sitting on the edge of the bed, watching him, she marveled at how casually Dan walked into the room, as if this day was like every other. Not knowing that this day would change his life forever. She enjoyed being the one who knew, not yet ready to share. She imagined she would think of some romantic and magical way of telling him, perhaps sliding the small sonogram image toward him at the end of a candlelit dinner.

They walked downstairs and began preparing dinner together while he talked about his day; the legal case he was working on, the weather, traffic, and she watched him like a Cheshire Cat, her smile there, then disappearing, until she could stand it no longer. "Honey," she began, "I have something to tell you." His skeptical nature jumped right to the dark side and his mood made a quick shift from all-is-well to maybe not.

"I knew it was unusual for you to be napping during the day," he began, "tell me there's nothing wrong, tell me you're okay." Standing up and walking to his side, Annie assured him she was fine, even better than fine. "You sit right here," she said as she guided him to the couch in the kitchen, "I have to get some evidence," smiling and emphasizing the last word.

Before she left the kitchen, she walked to the wine cooler, selected a bottle of their favorite Riesling, and poured one glass. I'm going to miss a glass of wine at the end of the day she thought. I can see myself now, in six months I'll be sipping Riesling while balancing diapers and baby food, she laughed. Returning to Dan she placed the filled wine glass on the small coffee table in front of him. "I'll be right back," she assured him. As for Dan he was lost, didn't have a clue about what was going on.

When she returned, she sat next to him and said, "Close your eyes and hold out your hands." Fortified by half a glass of wine, he obeyed. After placing the photo of their child into his open hands, she sat back and simply said, "Open." Obediently he opened his eyes and looked down. "What's this?" he asked, sounding like the typical person not yet introduced to the wonderful world of obstetrics. "Look more closely," she encouraged him.

Finally he held it up to the reading lamp next to the couch thinking that might shed more light on the subject. Then she saw it; his face lit up, his eyes grew larger, he began to shake his head back and forth, "No, this can't be what, or rather who, I think it is," he said incredulously. Then Annie began the story. Told him about the doctor's appointment that morning, assured him Carol believed she and the baby were fine, then she waited for his questions.

"How is this possible?" he asked no one in particular. "Carol herself told us we would never have children." "I asked her the same question this morning," Annie chimed in. "And?" Dan asked. "She said she has no idea how it's possible, but that she stands corrected." Then they laughed, holding onto each other, careful not to bend or wrinkle their only proof that their greatest wish had been answered.

# 26

James was walking out of the Burn Unit when Kathryn got off the elevator. When she saw his tear-stained face she stopped and held her breath. As soon as he saw Kathryn, he walked directly to her and took her hands. "It's okay," he assured her. "Grace is doing okay." Exhaling she asked what had happened. He could not tell her the truth, so implied that the situation had finally gotten to him. He told her he was on his way home where he hoped to take a long nap while the girls were at school.

Reassured, Kathryn walked him to the elevator, and then returned to the all-too-familiar waiting room. It had been two days since Gracie's accident. Kathryn wasn't sure why she was sitting there, she knew they wouldn't allow her to visit with Grace, but there was some comfort in knowing that one of Gracie's friends was standing guard.

Reaching into the pocket of her coat, she pulled out the paperback book she stuffed in there when she left the house that morning. Along with the book, an envelope floated out and drifted slowly down to the gleaming hospital floor. Caroline's note to Grace, she thought.

I had forgotten all about it. She studied the stained envelope as she picked it up.

The flap was opened. She could read it and no one would know. None of my business, she thought as she slid the note back into her pocket. I'll let James read it to Grace when she's feeling better. A half hour later Kathryn gave into temptation, retrieved the envelope, lifted the flap, and slid out the water-stained note.

"Dear Gracie –

I am so glad to be able to finally tell you this. We've never had secrets from each other and I know you will understand. This will clear the air and make everything better between us.

*(dear god, Kathryn thought.)*

Remember the night of the snow storm a few years ago when you asked James to stop at my house on the way home because you were worried when I didn't answer the phone? I don't know why you worried; you know I do that sometimes. Anyway, when James arrived, there was a blizzard outside. Remember he called you and you told him to stay at my house for the night?

James was very upset that night, Gracie. After a few drinks he told me he had made a few bad investments and lost most of your savings. He was afraid to tell you that if it were not for the money you earned as a substitute teacher, you guys would lose the house. I told him I had tons of money and would be more than happy to help, hell, I'd even pay up the mortgage, you know that, but he said you wouldn't even consider the possibility. I felt so sorry for him, Gracie.

Honestly, I don't remember much more about that night, we both had a lot to drink, but the next morning when I woke, he was sleeping beside me in my bed. As soon as I saw him, I got up and threw on a robe.

*(Kathryn stopped reading. Caroline had made many bad choices since Jack died, she thought, but nothing quite this despicable, and for some insane reason she decided this would be the perfect time to share this story with Grace. As for James, the bastard, she wasn't totally surprised. There was something about him that never rang true. She continued reading.)*

"James was so mad that morning, Gracie. He was afraid you would find out and we both know he couldn't make it without you. He made me promise I would never tell you. I'm breaking that promise now because you and I shouldn't have any secrets and I know you'd want to know what happened. So that's the whole story, Gracie. Don't be mad, it didn't mean a thing and we both love you very much. Caroline."

*(Son of a bitch)*

# 27

Kathryn grabbed her coat and stormed out of the Medical Center waiting room. She could feel the blood rushing through her veins and her ears were ringing. She was a woman who seldom got angry, but when she did everyone that knew her battened down the hatches until the storm blew over.

Her old station wagon actually squealed when she pulled out of the Medical Center parking lot. She barely noticed the stop lights on New Scotland Avenue and maneuvered through the roads in Albany's Washington Park in a way that definitely would have attracted the attention of Albany Police had there been a police car in the area. She didn't catch a red light driving down State Street then swung onto Rt. 787 at the Palace Theater. The morning traffic into Troy had dissipated on the Menands Bridge and left nothing to slow her down. She didn't catch the red light at the foot of Campbell's Avenue, allowing her to maintain her just-over-the-speed-limit forward motion.

At the top of Campbell's she made a quick left turn onto Maple Avenue, following it across Pawling, and continuing on Maple until she pulled the wheel sharply to the right onto Pinewoods. She parked the old wagon on the gravel driveway of the second house on the left and slammed the car door behind her before stomping up the wide front steps.

She used her key to open the front door, slammed it behind her, and yelled, "Caroline! Where are you? I want to speak with you now! What the hell were you thinking?"

For her part, Caroline was asleep until she heard the heavy front door slam against the doorframe and rattle the whole house. She was more angry than afraid; whoever was making the racket was causing her head to throb and interrupting the sleep she needed to end the symptoms of that morning's hangover. Before she could tie the robe around her waist, Kathryn came storming through the bedroom door and what a sight she was.

Her unbuttoned raincoat flew behind her like wings, clenched fists hung at each side, her eyes were bulging in her red face, the pupils dilated, and even the tops of her ears were red. She rushed up to Caroline and threw a piece of paper at her with such force that Caroline shrank from it. "Your best friend," Kathryn screamed, "Your best friend's husband, how could you? Don't you dare hide behind the bottle this time you, you ..." Kathryn could not finish. Caroline had no idea what Kathryn was screaming about until she looked at the wrinkled letter on the floor. "Oh, my god," was all she could say.

"That's right, oh, my god," Kathryn mimicked her. "It is despicable enough that you slept with your best friend's husband, but to choose this time to confess your sins, when Gracie is at her most vulnerable is reprehensible, even for you." "I thought I dreamed about writing that letter," Caroline said as much to herself as to Kathryn, "when I got up the next morning it was gone." Then it occurred to her, "How did you get your hands on that letter?" "I came by that morning to check up on you and found it next to you on your dining room table. I thought it was a sweet gesture on your part and stuck it in my coat pocket before it was misplaced."

Seeing an escape from the guilt, Caroline took it. She pulled herself up, stuck her chin in the air, and said, "You had no right to take that letter from my house. If you had minded your own business, this wouldn't have happened." "Don't you dare try to shift the blame to me," Kathryn shot back. "The world is full of men you can have sex with, yet you chose the husband of your best friend. What does that say about you, what does it say about James? To me, it says that neither of you deserve Grace in your life."

"You cannot tell Grace," Caroline said, panic rising in her voice now. Reaching down she snapped up the shriveled letter and tore it into small pieces, letting them drop to the floor like twirling whirligigs in autumn. "Me?" Kathryn snapped back. "Me? You think I would tell Grace your dirty little secret? I could never hurt her like that. But I want you to know," she continued, "that you have spent any last currency between you and me. You are on your own. I have always felt an obligation toward you, Caroline, to keep you safe for Jack's sake, but even Jack could not forgive you this time," she finished.

Turning on her heels, Kathryn stormed out of the room and out of the house. Five minutes after Kathryn's car pulled out of the driveway, Caroline still stood where Kathryn had left her.

# 28

A week had gone by since Grace's accident and Hedy didn't feel as compelled to be at the hospital every day. Instead, she decided to take advantage of a sunny, warmer Saturday and walk to the Atrium Mall in downtown Troy to do a little shopping. Afterward, as she walked back home, she marveled at how the winter weather in the Northeast could change overnight from fierce and bitter cold to blue skies and sunshine. The noontime sun was busy melting through the layers of ice that had accumulated on the gutters attached to the roofs of the century old brownstones surrounding her. Long dripping daggers of melting ice clung to the sides of the buildings and streams of water slithered like snakes on the ground below moving over and under melting snow banks searching for the nearest storm drains, only to fall once again into rushing water and travel beneath the city before tumbling into the Hudson River.

She heard her phone ringing when she reached the bottom step of her front porch but didn't rush to answer it, choosing instead to linger outside in the warmer weather. By the time she was inside and unpacking her shopping bag, the phone began to ring again. "Hello," she spoke into the clunky black receiver. An unfamiliar voice replied, "Hedy?" "Who is this, please?," she responded in the tone of voice she learned from her mother. "This is Steve Devan," he said. Again her mother's voice came out of her mouth, "I'm sorry, but I don't know you." "Oh, Dr. Devan from Albany Medical Center," he clarified. "Dr. Devan?" she repeated into the phone. "Yes, Grace's doctor."

"Is Grace okay?" she asked quickly. "Yes, nothing has changed," he responded. Relieved all was well, Hedy asked, "What can I do for you?" "Well, I was hoping, if you didn't have plans, that we could have dinner tonight. I know it may seem a bit odd, since I'm Grace's physician, but you're not the patient or a family member so I'm pretty sure it would be appropriate. What do you say?"

Hedy had been on only a few dates since Christopher died, including one terribly awkward evening she spent with a high school acquaintance she met at a class reunion. She had actually surrendered to the notion that her dating days were over, which meant she was totally unprepared to deal with his request. "Tonight?" she asked. "Yes, I know it's last minute, but I'm not on call tonight and we doctors have to grab the opportunity to socialize when we can. We both have to eat dinner, right? Why not let me pick you up and take you to my favorite Troy restaurant. Do you like Verdiles in the Burgh?" "Yes, it's a favorite of mine too. Every time I go there I promise myself to order something other than chicken parmesan, but I can't help myself," she said, knowing she was rambling.

"Do we have a plan then?" he asked. "Just a casual

dinner, who knows, we may end up being friends," he chided. "I can always use a new friend," Hedy replied. "Sure, why not." "Wonderful, how about I pick you up at 6? Now tell me where to find you."

Hedy hung up the phone after giving him directions. He said he knew her neighborhood. Colleagues of his had a practice just a block or two away from her house. She resisted telling him they were her doctors, figuring it was much too soon in their friendship to begin a conversation about her gynecologists.

Should I have said no, thank you, after all it was such short notice. Will he think I'm too eager, too needy? What does one wear on a date nowadays? Is it a date? Am I being presumptuous? Oh, hell, I'm too old for this, she thought.

Five hours later she sat in the formal parlor of her house nursing a chilled glass of wine. She worried that the black wrap around dress she wore was too formal, maybe she should have gone with a pair of slacks and a sweater. What if he showed up wearing something ultra-casual? The doorbell made her jump. Before she got up to answer it, she counted to twenty-five. Don't want him to think I'm too eager, she thought. She checked her hair in the hall mirror and wiped her damp palms on her dress before opening the heavy wood door.

Her first thought was, thank god, he's wearing a dress shirt and tie.

# 29

Hedy was enjoying the evening with Steven. When he arrived, he insisted that she invite him inside so he could have a tour of the house. He checked out every nook and cranny. "I love this place," he declared. "This is where I grew up," Hedy said as she watched his eyes flit from the decorative ceiling to the shiny hardwood floors. "All original details, I assume," a statement rather than a question. "Repaired over the years," she assured him, "but, yes, all original." He even swung the heavy wood front door back and forth a few times as they left.

Parked at the curb was his forest green Range Rover, reminding her of a TV program she had watched recently about the estates of England's royal family where they all drove Range Rovers. After he helped her climb into the passenger seat, she couldn't resist saying, "I've never been inside a Range Rover before but if it's okay for the royal family, then I guess it will do." "I know," he said sounding a bit embarrassed. "It's a splurge. I don't buy a lot of stuff but when I do find something I like, I go for it," he said smiling in Hedy's direction. She felt a butterfly take flight in her stomach.

Conversation came easy for them. He talked about

his upbringing on a dairy farm outside of Syracuse, New York. After high school he won a full scholarship to Cornell. At the time he thought he wanted to be a veterinarian, after all, don't most kids raised on a dairy farm want to be a vet at one time or another? Half way through his first year at Cornell, his biology professor saw something special in him and began to encourage him to consider medical school. And, as he said, "The rest is history."

"Why a burn specialist" Hedy asked. He gave her a wry smile then told his story. "I did my internship at UCLA Medical Center. You understand, the farm boy who wanted to see California," he smiled. "During the last year of my internship there was a fire on the farm. At the time dad had the largest dairy barn in New York State. The barn burned to the ground and all of the newly purchased, top-of-the-line milking equipment and over 200 Guernsey cows went with it. Dad, being the man he was, couldn't stand by and watch everything he had worked for his entire life go up in smoke, so he entered the burning barn multiple times and managed to save a dozen calves as well as assorted cats and the family dog."

"It wasn't until after the fire was out that mom got a good look at dad. His hands and face were badly burned. The emergency medical staff on standby at the farm took him immediately to the nearest hospital. That's when I got the call to come home." As the memories flooded in, his facial expression changed from one of pride for his father to wistfulness.

"Before I left UCLA I tracked down the best burn specialist on staff and he kindly agreed to call the small rural hospital where dad was a patient. He told me what to look out for when I arrived and how to approach the hospital staff. I went charging into the hospital on my white horse to rescue dad, but it was too late. Infection had already set in, his breathing was labored and by then transferring him to a medical center was out of the question. The medical staff did the best they could, it wasn't their fault that dad died. His burned hands had touched so many infectious materials while rescuing the animals that infection was inevitable."

He stopped and filled up her wine glass, then poured a bit more Syrah into his glass before continuing. "I went back to UCLA after the services. My brother Jim and his wife, Jeanne, had been working the farm alongside dad for a few years already, so they moved into the big house with mom and continued working the farm. Jim and Jeanne retired to Florida a few years ago and I bought them out. Which means now I am the proud owner of a quickly deteriorating piece of farm property in upstate New York." He finished with a self-mocking lilt to his voice.

"So you ended up specializing in burns because of your dad?" Hedy wanted to know. "Basically," he responded. "It's such a misunderstood injury. If protocols are followed in severe burn cases chances of survival are good, it's when the attending medical staff are unsure that things do not turn out so well. Many burn victims manage to survive their injuries, but cannot overcome the depression caused by the changes in their appearance. The psychological injuries are almost as important as the physical ones. Well, enough about me tell me more about you."

So she did and had just finished the part of her story that dealt with her life with Christopher when Steven's pager began to buzz. Looking extremely put-out he removed the pager from his belt and apologized before excusing himself to find a phone. A few minutes later he reappeared and apologized again, but told her there was a medical emergency and he needed to get to Albany Med as soon as possible. "I'll call a taxi," Hedy offered. "No, I'll drive you home, it's on my way," he responded, although he was clearly distracted.

When they got to Hedy's house, he walked her to the front door and almost got away before she asked him the one question he was dreading: "It isn't Grace, is it?"

# 30

Steven parked the Range Rover in his designated parking space just outside the Emergency Room door. Since his dad's death he had charged into hospitals on his white horse to rescue thousands of people and most times he was able to pull them through. He could repeat the names and birthdates of every patient that he lost and prayed he would not have to add Grace to that list.

When he responded to the page at the restaurant, the nurse spoke the "F" word, the last word he wanted to hear spoken in the same sentence with the name of any of his patients, "Fever." At last check Grace had a fever of 101, an hour before her temperature was normal.

During the elevator ride to the Burn Unit, he closed his eyes and took deep breaths followed by slow exhales. He needed his mind to be clear and focused. There was no one at the nurses' station when he stepped off the elevator. Walking quickly he reached the door of the Burn Unit, walked in, and then went directly to the small changing room where he donned protective clothing and washed up in the small stainless steel sink.

While he was drying his hands, the in-charge nurse walked in and began reading Grace's chart. Grace's fever was at 101.8. She had checked Grace's bandages and, based on her observations, believed the infection was in the muscle in Grace's right knee, the area that had suffered 4th degree burns. He continued listening as they walked toward Grace. Rather than rewrapping, the nurses had simply covered the knee area with sterile gauze, anticipating Steven's imminent arrival.

The muscle was swollen and red and appeared to be the center of the infection. He made a quick check of all Grace's burn sites, and then asked the nurse to get Grace's husband, James, on the phone.

Steven began to steel himself for the conversation. After all of the years he had been having these difficult discussions with patients' loved ones he had never conquered the feeling of anxiety that crept into his chest. The only way he could focus was to disassociate from the emotions involved and concentrate on the medical procedures being considered.

"Hello, James," he began, "I'm sorry to bother you at this late hour, but there has been a change in Grace's condition and we need to discuss how to move forward. Whatever we decide, I need your permission to proceed." "What? What's happened?" James voice shook. As calmly as he could, Steven told James about the fever, that the source of the infection was in the muscle of her badly burned right knee. Taking a breath, he told James that he needed to operate immediately in order to find out how much of the muscle tissue was involved and whether the infection had moved to the bone of her knee cap. He explained he would remove the infected muscle tissue and then with proper antibiotic therapy quell the infection.

"I have to rely on your expertise and experience," James replied. "When will you do the surgery?" "Right now if I have your permission," Steven responded. "And there is one more thing you need to know," he continued. "Yes? What is it?" "If I find osteomyelitis, if the bone is infected, or there is dead bone tissue, the tissue may have to be removed in order to prevent sepsis, which can be a life-threatening inflammation of the entire body caused by infection. Grace's immune system is compromised now and infections can spread quickly. Depending on what we have to do, removing bone tissue may cause Grace to be permanently disabled. I don't mean to scare you, James, but the reality of the situation is that we need to move quickly." "Okay," was James only response.

"James," Steven continued, "I know this is all overwhelming, but you have to concentrate on what I'm telling you right now. While I am not anticipating this outcome, if the infection has spread farther than I think it has, there is a very remote possibility that we may have to remove a section of Grace's leg." James gasped, "No, no, you do not have my permission to do that." "I understand," Steven responded (and he truly did), "you do not have to make that decision right now, but you do have to give all of this serious thought. I will begin the procedure and if and when we need to make further decisions, we will discuss everything first and I will answer all of your questions."   "Yes," James gasped, clearly relieved.

"How soon can you get to the medical center?," Steven asked.  "I'll call my sister to stay with the girls and as soon as she gets here, I'll leave.  I should be there in an hour." "Good," Steven replied.  "We'll begin at our end and by the time you arrive, we will know more."

# 31

While waiting for his sister to arrive, James called Kathryn, unfortunately for Kathryn. There were two people walking on the face of the earth that she did not want to talk to; James was one of them. Yet, his news was so upsetting that his tryst with Caroline seemed trivial in comparison. He began with, "I don't know what to do, Kathryn, the doctor wants to amputate Grace's leg."

"What? Slow down, James, what are you talking about?" "The older doctor just called and told me he was going to operate on Grace's knee, there's an infection, and he may have to amputate her leg." "You didn't give him permission to do so, did you?" Kathryn asked, afraid to hear the answer. "No, I did not. I'm on my way to the hospital as soon as Mary gets here to watch the girls. Dr. Devan said he would start the surgery and by the time I arrived he'd know more." Thank god, she thought. "Okay, James, I'll get dressed and meet you at the hospital; would you like that?" "Yes, please Kathryn, I was hoping you would say that, I don't know what to do." "Fine, I'll be there in 45 minutes," she assured him and hung up the phone.

What an ass he is, Kathryn thought, I'll be damned

if he is going to make any such decisions about Grace by himself. She immediately called Hedy, gave her a quick rundown on what was happening, and asked her to meet her at the medical center as soon as she could get there. "Oh, and call Annie, Hedy, and ask her to come to the medical center as well. We may need a good lawyer."

By the time James arrived at the waiting area outside the operating rooms, Kathryn, Hedy and Annie were sitting in the corner with their heads together. He had to walk up to them and say hello before they noticed him. Legally they could not intervene in any decisions that James might make, so they agreed to be as supportive as possible and if they felt he was going in the wrong direction, they would try to dissuade him and point out more acceptable alternatives.

It was a few minutes past 1 a.m. when James arrived at the medical center. An hour later there was still no word from the medical staff. Gracie's Tribe sat quietly listening to the beating of their hearts, praying, remembering, and hoping.

Shortly after 2:30 a.m., a very weary Steven walked into the waiting area, a blue surgical cap pushed back on his head. "Grace is doing well," he assured the four anxious faces looking up at him like newly hatched birds waiting to be fed. Sitting in a nearby chair, he pulled the surgical cap off his head and let it dangle between his opened legs. "We removed the infected muscle tissue and after checking all of the nearby bone tissue, we are confident the infection has not spread. We have closed her incision and there will be no further surgery tonight." In response to a choirs of "thank yous" and "great job," Steven raised his hands and cautioned. "This does not mean that Grace is out of the woods. During surgery her fever rose to 103.1. Now we wait and let the antibiotics and her system do their job. What we want is the fever to break. It could go up even higher as the night progresses. We hope to see it start to fall within the next few hours."

"And, if it doesn't?" James asked. "We'll deal with that if and when we have to," was Steven's wise reply. "I will keep you up-to-date," he told James, and then he stood up, told them all to go home and get some rest, threw a brief smile in Hedy's direction, and left.

# 32

Annie, Kathryn and Hedy left the medical center together, helped each other find their cars in the brightly lit parking lot, hugged each other good-bye, and drove away. Each woman exhausted, each relieved.

Dan didn't want Annie to drive to the medical center that night. Hedy's phone call woke them both and it was dark, cold, and damp outside. He counseled her to stay home, suggesting her friends could call her if a legal issue presented itself. In Annie's mind there was no question. Of course, she would go; Gracie needed her.

During the four hours Annie was away, Dan was restless. He worried about Grace, he worried about Annie, and he worried about their baby. Hell, he thought, I've known about our baby for such a brief period of time and already I'm worried about him or her. When Annie pulled into the back parking area, he breathed a sigh of relief and met her at the kitchen door. He helped her off with her coat and sat her down on the sofa where he removed her damp boots as she brought him up-to-speed on Grace's condition. He offered a warm cup of tea, but Annie was too tired. She thanked him for the offer, excused herself, dragged herself up the stairs, threw herself on the bed, and drifted off to a deep sleep.

When Kathryn drove into her driveway, she saw the light on in the kitchen and knew that meant John was awake. He opened the front door for her and took her coat. "Well, how is everything?" he asked. "Good, good," Kathryn replied, then explained what had happened at the medical center. "That sounds hopeful," he said, "certainly a better situation than you expected when you left." "I know," Kathryn replied wearily.

"How's James holding up?" John asked, then immediately noticed "The" look spread over Kathryn's face then disappear. He had seen that look a thousand times during their marriage and understood it was not a good thing. "What?" he coaxed her, "What's going on?" Maybe it was the hour, maybe it was because she was so tired, and maybe she just needed to tell someone what she knew, but the uncensored story of the letter, of the night Caroline and James spent together poured out of her mouth.

John was horrified. She knew that would be his reaction. Even if she woke up one morning looking like Medusa, snakes and all, he would honor his marriage vows and expected nothing less from all his married friends. He had witnessed all of Caroline's indiscretions over the years and forgave them in his way because he empathized with her, he understood the loss she was feeling but he loved Grace like a daughter and was angry at James for this betrayal.

Of course, there was nothing they could do with their anger and frustration. With Grace in the hospital and her daughters coping as best they could, now was not the time to call James out on his actions. So, they complained and commiserated with each other before climbing the stairs where they put on their pjs, and climbed into bed. Outside the morning sun was beginning to light up the sky.

It was still dark when Hedy drove up to her brownstone, but she had to park a block away because neighbors had taken advantage of her absence and pulled their second car into "her" spot. This happened every now and then, a downside of city living. At least she was able to park below a street light. She ran down the short block, then up the brownstone steps with her key poised and ready to unlock the door. Once inside she pulled off her boots, slid into her slippers, and padded her way down the hall to the kitchen.

There was so much to think about. So much had happened during the last twenty-four hours. She busied herself preparing a cup of warm tea and along with the first sip came a sense of relief that radiated through her body pushing a sigh out of her mouth. Grace was okay for now. She would hold on to that and try not to worry about what the next phone call might bring. And what about Steven; one minute he was her dinner date, charming her with his self-effacing stories, the next he was the man in charge, the doctor saving her dear friend's limb and possibly her life.

She sat at the old aluminum table from her childhood with her left elbow on the tabletop, her left hand under her chin supporting her head.  She must have nodded off because her elbow slipped and she caught her balance before falling off the old yellow vinyl chair.  Time to go to bed, she reminded herself as she stood up, brought the empty tea cup to the sink, climbed the stairs, and fell into bed.  She was asleep before her head hit the pillow.

# 33

The first signs of daylight were at the horizon when James turned into his driveway that night. The house was dark except for the light in the kitchen window. He looked at his watch to see how much time he had before the girls woke and would want him to tell them the latest news about Grace. He looked up just in time to avoid crashing into the back of Caroline's car.

Oh, no, just what I need right now, he thought as he slowed down, looking to see if Caroline was still in the car. The last thing he wanted to deal with was drunk Caroline in his living room. As soon as he came alongside the Mercedes, Caroline jumped out and into the passenger seat of his car. "What the hell are you doing here at this hour?" he spat out. "Where have you been?" she shot back. Since she was purposely left out of the loop about the recent change in Grace's condition, she was shocked when James explained what had happened.

"Why didn't anyone call me?" she asked the windshield. Although they both knew the answer, "I don't know," was James reply. "It's Kathryn," Caroline continued without even registering James' response, "she's really mad at me. I've never seen her angry like this before. I'm sure she's angry at you, too," she finished. "Me? Why me?" he wanted to know. He understood why Kathryn wouldn't want drunk Caroline at the hospital, but why would she be angry at him?

"She knows," was her simple reply. "She read the letter and she knows." Now he was getting mad. He was too tired to participate in this drunken nonsense. "I don't know what the hell you're talking about, Caroline. Why don't you get back in your car and go home? It's late, the girls will be up in a few hours and I need to sleep."

"She knows we had sex," she blurted out. "You told her?," he asked incredulously. I thought we agreed that was our secret, when did you tell her?" "I didn't tell her," Caroline defended herself and then told him about the letter she wrote to Grace and how Kathryn had taken the letter and read it. After taking a bit of time to digest the story, James said, "Well, she hasn't said anything to me about a letter. Are you sure you're not imagining the whole thing?" "Oh, no, she came storming into my house and ripped a strip off of me, she said horrible things to me, and I don't think she will ever speak to me again."

James' mind began to race. He knew why Kathryn hadn't said anything to him. It was because of Grace and the girls. He began to break out in a sweat wondering what Kathryn would do when Grace had recuperated. Then his selfish little mind kicked into gear and he began to wonder why this was happening to him. One small indiscretion with drunk Caroline and his world could change forever. It was all drunk Caroline's fault.

He ordered Caroline out of his car, "Get out now," he demanded. His mind was forming a plan, "This is all your fault, you knew what you were doing when you kept pouring that Scotch, you wanted me to sleep with you so you would have something to hold over Grace's head. You've always been jealous of her." Caroline was incredulous. "Me? If I weren't drunk, I never would have slept with you, James. Grace is my best friend." He, of course, could not resist taking her last statement and hitting her over the head with it. "Ha, some best friend you are, sleeping with your best friend's husband." "But you ..." Caroline began, but her liquor addled mind couldn't form the thought.

Resembling a battered child, Caroline slinked away and quietly locked herself inside her car and drove off. James watched her taillights disappear at the end of the driveway before getting out of his car and walking into the house. He was so busy developing a defense for his actions that he didn't see his ten year old daughter, Abigail, watching him and her "aunt" Caroline from the upstairs window.

# 34

When she regained consciousness, Grace's first thought was, now what? She had figured out there had been an accident and whatever had happened had left her incapacitated and in serious pain. She remembered James and their girls.

She was alone in the room now. It was quiet and she could hear her heartbeats echoing back at her from the machine beside her head.

Her dressing gown was soaking wet. The sensation reminded her of when she was a child, sick with one illness or another, and the fever broke. She recognized she was feeling better, but the pain had not subsided and now there was a different kind of pain in her left knee.

For the first time she was able to slowly turn her head a few inches and could see there were no other patients in the large room. In the distance she saw a large glass door and could almost make out the lettering ... T I N U N R U B. That makes absolutely no sense, she thought. Must be the drugs; Alice in Wonderland has nothing on me.

She wondered if she was getting used to the pain, or if it was beginning to subside. It still hurt like hell, but she was tolerating it better than she had before. She tried to raise her arms but they felt like lead, so she turned her thoughts to remembering her girls' faces when it suddenly dawned on her.

TINUNRUB ... BURN UNIT! "Oh, my god, I'm in the Burn Unit," she cried out. "What happened?" Then she remembered James backing away, his tears, the chair turned over. What do I look like? By then the nurses had noticed the change in Grace's heartbeat and rushed to her bedside. "What happened?" she asked them, "Please, tell me." "Am I grotesque?" "Please get me a mirror." Grace began to struggle to sit up and kept repeating, "I need a mirror, please get me a mirror," she begged until one of the nurses disappeared and came back with a large mirror that she held in front of Grace's face.

"Thank god," Grace whispered when she saw her reflection. Although it was a face filled with fear, it was her face, unchanged. "What happened," she asked. "Where am I burned?" "Rest now," one of the nurses soothed her as she settled the pillows under her head. We've just given you something to help you sleep. The doctors will explain everything to you soon." Grace resisted, "But I don't want to sleeee ..."

# 35

Two days after the knee surgery, Dr. Steven Devan sat in a chair at Grace's bedside and explained everything that had happened to her. He began with the accident. Grace listened as an interested bystander; she could not remember the boiling water, the pan catching on the sleeve of her robe, or the helicopter ride to the medical center. Steven assured her that many patients who experience traumatic injuries do not remember the event. It's the brain's way of shutting the memory out until the body is able to cope.

Then he described her burns, where they were located, and his prognosis for her recovery. Her left breast was badly burned as was her stomach, pelvic area, left thigh and the tops of her feet. As he spoke Grace's imagination went into overdrive and she began to panic at the images her mind created. "We have already completed seven surgeries, Grace," he continued, "Four were skin grafts. You will not lose your breast and it should heal with minimum scarring. All signs indicate your body has accepted the skin grafts we've done so far."

He forged ahead, "Your left knee has caused us the most concern. The burn moved down into the muscle and caused an infection. We had to operate a few days ago to remove the infected tissue around your knee." Grace wanted him to stop; she couldn't process it all, but she also wanted to understand what to expect. He continued, "Today there is no sign of infection and we are optimistic it will not return. We won't know for a while yet if there is permanent damage to your knee but, believe me, Grace, this is the very best scenario.

"What's important to understand here, Grace, is that you are one of the lucky ones. In many ways you are lucky to be alive and all indications are that you are on your way toward complete recovery. We expect that you will remain in the hospital for another few months. There will be additional surgeries, more skin grafts, and then when your body is ready, physical therapy. We will begin to decrease the amount of pain killers you are receiving. I'm sure you've heard how addictive they can be. On the other hand, please don't try to be noble about this; if you're in a lot of pain at any time, please ask for help."

"In a few weeks, when the risk of infection has subsided, you can begin to have visitors." To Grace's ears that was the best news she heard so far. "My girls," Grace began, "I want to see my girls, but I don't want them to be frightened by all of this," she said as her eyes scanned the room. "You know them better than anyone, Grace. If they're more sensitive, it may be best to wait until you're sitting up and feeling better. I'll leave that up to you and James."

"I suspect that's quite enough information for today,"

Steven said as he stood up and moved the chair out of the way. "I'm sure, as we move forward, you'll have hundreds of questions and we want you to ask them, don't be shy. Do you have anything you'd like to know right now? Are you comfortable?" "Actually, I'm feeling very tired and need to sleep." "Good, Grace, sleep will help you heal. I'll check in on you in the morning."

# 36

Three weeks later Abigail struggled with the twins as she tried to prepare them for their first visit with Grace in the medical center. They refused to sit still when she tried to brush through the knots in their hair. They argued with her about which dress they would wear and refused to eat the tuna sandwiches Abigail made for lunch. Unfortunately for the twins, Abigail was a worthy opponent who was accustomed to their attempts to join forces and wear her down. She simply told them they would have to stay home if they didn't cooperate. Since the newness of Grace's daily absence had worn off and the twins were anxious to see her, they surrendered and sat for the brushing, nibbled at the tuna, and climbed into the dresses Abigail had chosen.

Once they were presentable, Abigail sat them down on the living room sofa and reminded them they could not run to their mother and hug her. Her burns were still healing and it would be very painful if they did. If they saw any of their mom's burns, she told them not to make any comments that would make mom feel bad. At six-years old, the twins were prepared to see the same mom they were accustomed to and basically ignored Abigail's counseling.

As for Abigail, she was terrified. She had so many nightmares in which her mom was hideously disfigured that she wasn't sure she would be able to even get out of the car at the medical center, let alone go inside. Nevertheless, she helped the girls on with their boots, buttoned up their winter coats, and after pulling on her boots and coat, helped the twins climb into the back seat of their dad's car.

James had offered her the very grown up opportunity to sit in the front seat for the drive to Albany, but Abigail had refused and chose to sit in the back with the twins. Ever since that night a month before when she overheard her dad and Aunt Caroline arguing in the front yard, she had been avoiding any contact with her father by scooting away from the table right after dinner to wash dishes and then up to her room for homework and reading until bedtime. She didn't really understand what had happened between her dad and Aunt Caroline, she was only ten years old, but she knew sex was something that adults did, but only with the person they were married to and her dad had done it with Aunt Caroline. She could tell by the tone of their voices that night that they had done something wrong.

Before she was ready, the car pulled into the medical center parking lot. Abigail busied herself with calming down the twins and helping them out of the car. As soon as they walked inside the building, Dottie began complaining about the hospital smell and, since she was the drama queen of the family, began to gag. "Stop that," dad ordered before Dottie got carried away. Just the tone in his voice stopped the gagging.

The elevator ride was something new for the twins and they quietly watched the buttons light up and the tall metal doors open and close as people got on and off. They laughed and reached toward each other every time the elevator lurched upward, their knees buckling under them. When an orderly pushed a middle-aged man in a wheelchair onto the elevator they stepped backwards toward their dad like synchronized swimmers. Abigail watched the twins, but her thoughts were a few floors away, anticipating what she might see when she walked into her mom's hospital room. Her dad had assured her that Grace's face was uninjured during the accident, but Abigail had lost faith in her dad.

James herded the children toward the nurse's station when they got off the elevator. "We're here," he said cheerfully. "Well, hello," the nurse responded looking at the children. "Your mom is so excited to see you. Remember, don't jump on mom today. You can hold her hand if you want. Mom is still a bit stiff so she may not be able to reach down to kiss you today, but maybe dad can lift you up to her one at a time."

Somewhere between stepping off the elevator and meeting the nurse the twins became reticent. Wordlessly they nodded their heads in agreement with everything the nurse said and Abigail noticed they were holding hands.

Then the long walk down the hall towards Grace's room. Grace was no longer in the Burn Unit critical care area. Annie and Dan insisted on paying for a sunny private room, although Grace believed her health insurance plan was covering the extra cost.

Abigail was holding her breath and her shoulders were so tight they almost touched her ears. The twins and James stepped into Grace's room first. As soon as they saw Grace sitting in a chair next to her hospital bed, they rushed to her side with cheers of "mommy, hi, mommy, we came to see you; you've been gone a long time, when are you coming home?" Abigail stood in the doorway. She allowed her eyes to look at her mother's feet which were hidden in white socks and then let her eyes move up her legs which were hidden by a pale pink robe. When her gaze reached Grace's white and unscarred hands, she was so encouraged that Abigail quickly looked at her mother's face and almost fainted with relief when she saw her mother's beautiful white skin, her face exactly as she remembered it, smiling up at her. Her legs buckled and James reached to balance her.

"Come here, sweetie," Grace coaxed Abigail. "I've heard you are the woman of the house, taking care of everyone. I'm so proud of you," Grace continued, clasping Abigail's hands in her own. "You look the same, mom," Abigail blurted out. "I'm getting there, honey," Grace agreed.

And so, for the remainder of their visit, the small family sat together in a circle, the twins delighted to be lifted up to sit on "mommy's bed," Abigail and James on either side of Grace. The warm sun streamed through the window, bringing with it hope for an early spring. When the twins became fidgety, Grace suggested it was time for everyone to leave and reluctantly they said their goodbyes. Abigail was the last to leave the room.

# 37

Grace had two medical procedures during the week following her family's visit, including her 14$^{th}$ skin graft. As a result she was not up for visitors during that time. However, when Kathryn, Annie, and Hedy heard that Grace could have one visitor the following Sunday, Hedy suggested they flip a coin. Annie had another plan. She invited Kathryn and Hedy to dinner and after an evening filled with comfort food, roast chicken and garlic mashed potatoes, Annie sat her friends down in front of the blazing kitchen fireplace, poured them a fresh glass of wine and presented her case as to why she should be the first friend to visit Grace. She ended her defense by telling her friends that she was pregnant.

Annie had such a silly smile on her face, Hedy couldn't stop laughing at the news, assuming her friend had a bit too much wine and was pulling their leg. That is until she saw that Annie's wine glass was filled with ginger ale. Kathryn wasn't laughing. She believed Annie's news, but was shocked into silence. "I know, I know," Annie began. "The doctor is as surprised as we are since she's the one who assured us we would never have a child of our own."

Regaining her voice, Kathryn asked when the baby

would be arriving and exactly "how pregnant" was she? Annie's response of "almost five months" floored them again. "I know, I know," Annie continued. "You're both wondering why I kept it a secret for so long."

"First of all, I didn't know myself until I was three months pregnant. Remember when I went for the physical about six weeks ago? You were both pushing me to keep that appointment. I thought my symptoms were a result of being upset because of what happened to Grace but, after a few tests, Carol assured me I was indeed three months pregnant. You can imagine Dan's reaction.

Then, a few weeks after that, there was some spotting. Carol told me the spotting was caused by nothing more than what she called an incompetent cervix. When I told Dan, he said that was the first time he heard anyone refer to any part of me as incompetent. Once the spotting stopped, it took Dan and me a few weeks to get our balance back to the point where we're beginning to actually believe we will have this baby and now we are ready to tell our family and friends."

"What was your parents' reaction?" Hedy asked. "We haven't told them yet," Annie replied sheepishly. "You two are the first to know." Then she continued, "Here's the thing, I was hoping that you would agree to let me visit Grace on Sunday. Because you were not looking for it, you obviously haven't noticed the size of the shirt I'm wearing. I've already bought enough maternity clothes to fill my wardrobe. The waist bands on my clothes are so tight now I'll have to begin wearing maternity clothes soon. Before that I was hoping to see Grace so I could tell her about the baby. What do you think?"

"Of course," Hedy sputtered, "of course, you visit Grace on Sunday and give her my love. Better yet, I'm going to write Grace a note that you can bring with you." Kathryn rolled her eyes when Annie looked in her direction, "What some people will do to get their own way," she said, with a smile.

Annie's baby was a beacon of light for those three weary friends, a beautiful spring flower breaking ground after a long winter. Annie's baby was the counterbalance to long worrisome afternoons in hospital waiting rooms, to orchestrating meals and transporting Grace's girls to sports practice and dance classes, taking them clothes shopping, and to the hairdressers while reassuring them that their mommy was getting better and would be home soon, even if they were unsure of that themselves.

# 38

Annie walked down the long drab hall toward Grace's hospital room that Sunday afternoon stepping around a metal cart covered with small white paper cups holding a rainbow of carefully rationed pills. She tried not to listen to the whispered conversations drifting out of the doorways as she passed. Instead she concentrated on how to begin a conversation with Grace. They hadn't talked since before Grace's accident and so many things had happened in those two months, big, dramatic, life-changing things. Should she mention the accident? Should she hug her? Should she look at Grace's wounds if they were exposed? When and how should she tell Grace about the baby?

Then, there she was, standing in the doorway looking at Grace sitting in a chair facing one of the four narrow windows, her back to the door. The early April sun streamed through the windows creating shadows on the floor, bookends holding Grace in place. Annie thought Grace was sleeping and tip-toed closer. Slowly Grace turned her face in Annie's direction. "Annie, I'm so glad it's you," she said when she saw her friend. "James told me one friend could visit today, but he wouldn't tell me who it would be. Come here and give me a hug." Instead Annie froze in place, overwhelmed by the relief of seeing the friend she worried about for so long sitting there smiling and talking as though nothing had happened. Of course, there were tears, but Annie hadn't noticed. "Oh, stop that, and come here," Grace ordered. And so she did.

After hellos, Annie pulled up a chair and they stared at each other not sure where to begin. "You know I've always been a klutz," Grace admitted wryly. "Yes, I do know that," Annie agreed with a smile. "How are you Gracie? You look wonderful." "What you can see looks wonderful," Grace replied, "The rest, not so much but it's getting there. They've layered me with so much pig skin; I expect to start oinking any day now." And they were off, two friends in conversation, no topic a taboo.

Grace still did not remember the "event" as she called it. She had a vague recollection of a helicopter ride, but wasn't sure if it was a true memory or something she had seen on TV. The physical therapy to increase the elasticity in her joints was difficult, and the physical therapy for her left knee was a bear. She confided that although none of the medical staff would admit it, she secretly suspected she would always walk with a slight limp. She expected to be at the medical center for three or four more weeks and could not wait to go home to her girls.

Then Grace asked, "So, Annie, how are you? I have to tell you how good you look, so rested and relaxed. Have you cut back on that wicked work schedule of yours?" "Funny you should ask," Annie began. "Everything is okay, right?" Grace countered. "Actually better than okay, I'm pregnant." Grace blinked and furrowed her brow as though she didn't hear correctly. "I thought you said you were pregnant," Grace chuckled. "That's exactly what I said," Annie replied. "What? You are? How did that … well I know how it happened, of course, but what a surprise. When? When is the baby due?"

"The baby arrives in approximately four months, the end of July or early August." "Why didn't you tell me earlier?" Gracie asked. "I didn't know myself until after your accident and by then I was already three months pregnant." "How do you feel, how's the pregnancy going?," Grace asked. "I feel fine," Annie replied, "It's like this little person read the book and knows just what to do. I did have an amniocentesis done a few weeks ago and it will be another few weeks before we get the results but, honestly Grace, while we hope for a clean bill of health the results are almost inconsequential now that I can feel the baby moving. Dan and I are committed to this little person no matter what."

"I can't wait to see him or her, "Grace told her friend. "Hey, won't the amnio tell you the sex of the baby?" "Yes, and we've decided we do want to know, we simply cannot wait." "Neither can I," Grace added.

When they had exhausted all baby topics, Grace asked about her friends and wanted to know how Annie managed to become the first friend to visit. "The baby news, of course," Annie replied, "babies trump everything." Then she remembered, "Wait, I have a note from Hedy," she said while reaching into her coat pocket. "Hedy said we could read it together. Do you want me to?" "Sure," Grace replied.

"Dear Grace –

I want you to know that I hoped to be the first of your friends to visit, but "some people" will do anything, even what once seemed impossible, to get there first. Isn't it the most wonderful news? We're all going to be aunties.

We have all been monitoring your progress while keeping the seats warm in the medical center waiting room for the past two months. You are my hero, sweetie. I am so sorry this happened to you and so proud of how well you're doing. I've taken your girls to the movies a few times, G- rated only, of course, and the twins are handling your absence as only six-year olds can, seeing it all as a great adventure. Abigail, on the other hand, is more brooding as you well know, but that is her nature. I did notice a definite lightening of spirits after she was able to visit with you and see you for herself.

I'll let you two get on with your visit now. Know that I am looking forward to my turn to sit and chat with you. There is news to tell!

All my love,
Hedy"

"There is news to tell?" Grace asked her visitor. "Very good news," Annie replied, "but you'll have to wait so Hedy can tell you herself." Feigning disappointment, Grace acquiesced.

"And, Kathryn? How is she?" Annie smiled as she replied, "Stoic through this whole ordeal; she was the strong one who kept us all from falling apart. Now that she knows you are going to be okay, she has gone back to her shop. It's been interesting to watch how what you're going through seems to have made Kathryn and John closer somehow. You know how he drifted away when Jack was killed, and although she never talked about it, we all know how hurt she has been. Well, after all of this time, the old John is back. He's focused on Kathryn again and, damn, the woman is happy."

"I never thought he'd come back from that place," Grace said thoughtfully. "It's unfortunate I had to go through the tortures of hell to make it happen, but anything for my friends," she joked, that wry smile on her face again.

"And Caroline?" "The same … still drinking like a fish and abusing herself. Although something happened between her and Kathryn and from what I can tell Kathryn has washed her hands of Caroline again. This time Kathryn seems adamant and may not change her mind. When I tried to coax the details out of her, Kathryn would not talk about what happened. I haven't seen or heard from Caroline for almost two months now."

A frown creased Grace's brow, "Oh dear, that's not

good," she said. "Caroline is so fragile I can't imagine she'll be able to cope without knowing Kathryn will be there to pick her up." "Kathryn and you, sweetie," Annie reminded her, "but you have enough on your plate right now. Caroline will have to fend for herself."

# 39

During the almost two months since Kathryn stormed out of Caroline's house, Caroline had been avoiding the medical center, not wanting to cross paths with Kathryn again any time soon. A decision which made her feel even more isolated and alone. She also did not want to see James again after that humiliating early morning conversation in his driveway, so she substituted daily phone conversations with Hedy for hospital visits and Hedy kept her up-to-date on Grace's progress. Hedy assumed Caroline was avoiding the hospital because she didn't want to run into Kathryn and although she had no idea why the two women were not speaking to each other, she didn't really care. For the first time in a very long time, Hedy was having fun and enjoying her life and didn't want to get pulled into their drama.

When Hedy told her that Annie was going to be the first friend to visit Grace, it was the proverbial last straw as far as Caroline was concerned. She was Grace's oldest friend, she should be the person to visit Grace. After stewing about it for a few days, one damp, cold April morning, a tired and hung over Caroline decided to run away from home. That was her pattern; she spent her adult life running away from people and circumstances that made her feel anxious and uncomfortable. She never understood her friends' need to talk through problems when it was much easier to run away from them.

After a quick shower she threw on a pair of jeans and a warm black sweater then carelessly packed an overnight bag, tossing in a change of clothes and a few chilled bottles of vodka. With only a vague destination in mind, she drove up NY Route 2 toward Massachusetts. In the 15 minutes it took her to reach the small hamlet of Grafton, one of the two vodka bottles was already opened and a good percentage of its contents had been poured into a coffee mug, a rouse to prevent overzealous local police officers from investigating a suspicion.

At the foot of Petersburg Pass, the luxury car revved its engine like an angry bull and then charged up the steep winding hill. For her part, Caroline might just as well have been sitting in the passenger seat enjoying the panoramic views for all the attention she gave to the road ahead. Miraculously she made it to the top of the Pass and then charged down the other side toward Massachusetts, following the twisting road at breakneck speed.

She had a vague recollection that the Clark Art Museum was somewhere in the vicinity and followed her instincts for an hour or so before finally pulling into the museum parking lot. At this point she had consumed three "cups of coffee" poured from the bottle of vodka balanced precariously in the cup holder on the console between the front seats. She stepped out of the car and monitored her balance, locked the doors, and then walked toward the museum entrance.

For the next hour she wandered through the rooms of the museum, visiting her favorite paintings by Renoir, Monet, and Degas until she found herself sitting on a bench in front of John Singer Sargent's "Carnation, Lily, Rose." In the painting two young girls in white party dresses are studying paper Chinese lanterns in a summer rose garden. The painting mesmerized her, reminding her of her childhood with Grace. Like an old movie film speeding out of control, images from her childhood began to flash in her memory. Caroline had seen that film before, but this time the colors were darker, toys were broken, and the landscape surrounding her and Grace seemed threatening somehow.

The museum guard noticed the attractive woman sitting on the bench crying. He had seen it before, a visitor overcome by the beauty of a painting. Since she was one of just a dozen visitors that weekday, he left the room to give her privacy. When he returned ten minutes later, he was surprised to see the woman in the same place and felt compelled to ask if she was feeling okay. Looking through soupy eyes Caroline nodded yes, collected the handbag at her feet, and walked away.

After leaving the museum, Caroline stopped at the first motel she saw. She checked in and found Room 14 at the end of a long row of brightly painted doors. Once inside the modest room, she turned on the TV as loud as she dared, hoping the droning voices would distract her from the self-loathing accusations filling her head. Next she unscrewed the top of the second bottle of vodka, tore the protective paper from a clear plastic glass she found balanced on the bathroom sink, and poured the vodka into the glass until it reached the brim.

The hell with Grace, she thought, the hell with them all.

# 40

Caroline woke the next morning to the sound of rain pelting the window of the dark motel room. She rolled over and pulled the coarse bed cover over her head hoping to fall back to sleep, but the scent of strong cleaning chemicals drifting from the cover made her gag and rush to the tiny cold bathroom where she vomited into the bowl. Longing for the soft expensive towels she knew were hanging in her bath at home, she wiped her face with the motel's rough, washed-too-often-in-strong-detergent towel, and shuffled back toward the bed.

Her body tensed when she saw the toppled empty bottle of vodka on the night stand and realized it was the last of the lot she brought with her and that she'd never find a liquor store open this early in the morning. She began to putter, tossing her few toiletries scattered around the room into the overnight satchel, moving for motion's sake. The activity allowed her to believe the lie that comforted her, the absurd lie that she didn't need a drink, that she could stop drinking whenever she wanted.

Before long, anger began to creep in and, without liquor to tame it, grew quickly, a huge black bubble capturing Caroline inside. She was angry there wasn't a liquor store open, she was angry that it mattered to her, she was angry that it was pouring outside, that Kathryn was such a holier-than-thou-bitch, that Grace was so fucking clumsy, that something in the universe decided it was okay to leave an eight-year old Caroline alone in the world without her parents, and years later decided to take Jack from her, too.

By the time she tossed a ten dollar bill on the dresser and slammed the motel room door behind her, Caroline was furious at everyone she had ever known and every bad thing that ever happened to her. After walking through sheets of cold rain, she threw her overnight bag into the car where it bounced off the passenger door and rocked to a stop on the car floor, muffling the unmistakable sound of breaking glass. She assumed the $500 bottle of Jean Patou's Joy perfume that she picked up on her last New York City shopping spree had shattered inside the bag. She could have cared less. Unless the aroma became overpowering, which would then, of course, be one more offense to be angry about.

A sliver of yellow and gray was breaking at the horizon when she slammed her foot on the gas and spun out of the motel parking lot. At that hour of the morning there were only a few other cars on the road which allowed her to speed through the small Massachusetts towns dotting the highway. Punching the radio button, Janis Joplin's big voice boomed inside the Mercedes and Caroline sang along to the song she knew so well, laughing at the irony of the lyrics, "With them windshield wipers slapping time ..." Then, the refrain that always rang true to her, "Freedom's just another word for nothing left to lose ..." and at that moment, Caroline truly believed she had nothing left to lose.

She drove like a maniac down the wet and winding Petersburg Pass, moving from Massachusetts into New York State without noticing, all the while wondering what it would feel like to take the car airborne, to just break through a guardrail and take flight.

When she reached the small town of Petersburg at the bottom of the mountain, she noticed she had lost the '60s radio station and began to play with the radio dial. When she looked up, it was too late. She watched in horror as her 4000 lb. car hit the jogger on the side of the road, sending the unsuspecting runner ten feet into the air before landing in a crumpled heap on the front steps of a small home 30 feet away.

# 41

Annie and Dan were sound asleep when the phone on their bedside table began to ring that morning startling them awake. Dan reached over and picked up the receiver while Annie laid back and listened to the one-sided conversation. "Caroline, is that you? Are you okay?" Dan asked sympathetically. "What's going on?" He listened to Caroline's explanation and then said, "I'm sorry, Caroline, but I don't know about that; Annie is exhausted." He thought for a few seconds, then said a bit reluctantly, "I'll tell you what, I'll come instead; tell me where you are."

Annie rolled over and took the receiver from Dan's hand, ignoring the concerned look on his face. "Caroline, this is Annie, what's going on?" She listened in silence as Caroline haltingly described the accident. Annie assumed Caroline was drunk and asked if she had a breathalyzer test. "What? Oh, yes, they did give me one of those tests, Annie, but it came back okay." Without thinking, Annie replied incredulously, "It did? Are you sure?" "Yes, yes, I'm sure," Caroline snapped back. "Where are you?" Annie asked. "At the State Police station just outside of Petersburg. Will you come, Annie?

I'm really scared. You should have seen the poor guy I hit. He's in critical condition, in a coma ..." Caroline's voice trailed off.

"Yes, yes, of course, I'll come." Annie replied while Dan tapped her shoulder shaking his head. "I'll be there in an hour." When she hung up the phone, she looked at Dan. "I know, Dan," she began, "but I can't leave her there alone, not that she wouldn't appreciate you showing up, but she needs a friend right now, and with Kathryn not speaking to her, I've got to go. I went to sleep early last night, I'll be okay." "Well," Dan exhaled, "then I'm going, too. She's going to need all the legal help she can get." "Surprisingly, she passed the breathalyzer test," Annie told him, "at least she thinks she did." "Well, that is a surprise," Dan responded, "We'll see when we get there."

"Are you going to call Kathryn and John?" Dan asked from the large bedroom walk-in closet. "No, I don't think so," Annie replied from the bedroom bath. "Something's going on between Kathryn and Caroline. Kathryn can't seem to bring herself to even speak to her. Maybe Caroline has already called her. I'll see what's going on when I talk with Caroline."

Forty-seven minutes later Annie and Dan walked into the Petersburg State Police station. Caroline was sitting on a side chair at a desk. Her tear-stained face was as white as fresh snow. When she saw Annie and Dan standing in the doorway of the police station, she stood up and walked slowly toward Annie, then threw her arms around her neck and began to sob. Dan gently pulled her away and walked her back to the chair. The officer on duty, Captain Murray, introduced himself. Annie and Dan were stunned when they realized drunk driving was not an issue and that the State Police were calling it an accident caused by poor visibility in the rain.

"We have all the information we need," Captain Murray assured them. "You can take her home. Her car is in the parking lot behind the building. We've already taken photos of the damage. She can have a tow truck come by and pick it up. The insurance company will want to take a look."

When they asked how the jogger was doing, the captain shrugged his shoulders and shook his head. "Dom has been airlifted to Albany Medical Center in critical condition." "You know him?" Dan asked. "Sure, we all know Dom, he grew up here and is a fourth grade teacher at our grammar school." "Does he have a family, kids?" Dan flinched when he asked. "No, he's a single guy, but engaged, supposed to get married this spring." Annie was sympathetic, but her thoughts were stuck back on the phrase, "... air lifted to Albany Medical Center." Déjà vu, she thought.

Caroline was distraught during the drive home. Of course, she blamed herself and her damned temper. If she weren't so self-absorbed, she would have been paying attention to the road and the poor guy wouldn't be in a coma. Annie sat in the back seat with Caroline and held her hand, assuring her there would be no legal consequences. There may be a civil law suit in the future, but for now Caroline was out of the woods.

"If this poor man recovers, I will give him everything I own," Caroline blurted out. "I know that's how you feel right now, Caroline, but you do have to protect your interests. We'll discuss all of that in a week or so. Right now you're in shock and you need to go home and rest. Do you want me to call Kathryn and ask if she can stay with you?" Annie asked. "Kathryn? Hell no, I'm the last person she wants to spend time with. Don't call her at all. Just let it be." Annie was still curious about what was going on between Caroline and Kathryn, but knew it was neither the time nor the place for that conversation.

"Okay, okay," Annie assured her, "no Kathryn. How about Hedy? Shall I call her?" "Hedy," Caroline echoed, "yes, call Hedy please and thank you Annie, and you, too, Dan for coming to my rescue one more time. I can assure you this will be the last time anyone will have to bail me out of anything."

Dan looked in the rearview mirror and he and Annie rolled their eyes at each other.

# 42

Dominick Castaluccio never knew what hit him. His doctors did not expect him to survive his injuries and gave only minimal attention to his broken left femur and the fracture in his left arm once the surgery to patch the break in his skull was completed. For two weeks he lay in a coma, until one morning he opened his eyes and told the astonished nurse attending to him that he was hungry.

With the exception of the day she married Jack, the day Dominick regained consciousness was the happiest day of Caroline's life. Since the accident she had visited the hospital every day to check on Dominick's condition and, even more significantly, had not had a drop of liquor during that time. His family was surprisingly forgiving to Caroline, assuring her they did not blame her for the accident and that they had warned him about running in the bad weather that morning. Even so, Caroline gladly assumed responsibility for Dominick's medical expenses and asked his family to let her know if he or they needed anything.

One afternoon after Dominick had regained consciousness, Caroline was at the hospital chatting with his fiancé, Janet, when Janet mentioned that her brother Charlie was a Vietnam Vet. Charlie was sitting beside Janet and looked a bit embarrassed to be singled out. Caroline told him about Jack and how he had died in Vietnam 13 years before. "Are you Jack Gardiner's widow?" Charlie asked. To say Caroline was shocked would be an understatement. "Yes, yes I am." Caroline replied. "Did you know, Jack?" she asked.

"Yes, I did" Charlie replied with admiration. "Not well, he was in an entirely different outfit but we were introduced one night over there because someone noticed we were from the same area in upstate New York. We spent a few hours talking about back home over a couple of beers, but Jack was off on a mission the next day and I never saw him again. He talked about his Caroline and how anxious he was to get home."

"I'm speechless," Caroline responded, "I never imagined I would finally find someone who knew Jack when he was in Vietnam." "I can tell you this," Charlie continued, "Jack didn't die in Vietnam." "What?" Caroline gasped. "He died in Laos. The US has never admitted we had boots on the ground in Laos, but we were always moving troops near the Ho Chi Minh Trail, especially snipers like your Jack. I remember hearing Jack was killed near the trail in Laos and brought back into Nam by his buddies who refused to leave him there." Caroline was stunned. After all those years, she was finally hearing the truth about what had happened to her Jack.

"I'm sorry," Charlie apologized, "I didn't mean to

upset you but the least we can do is tell the truth to the families of the guys who went down over there." "No, no, I'm okay," Caroline assured him. "I'm happy to finally hear the truth about what happened to Jack." "Then you should know how respected he was by the men who fought beside him." "Thank you," was all Caroline could say.

When Caroline wasn't checking on Dominick's condition, she would ride the elevator up the two floors to Grace's room and spend time with her. In their conversations before Dominick regained consciousness, Caroline was contrite but not defensive or morose. When it became obvious Dominick would survive, Caroline seemed genuinely surprised and grateful that life had given her such a wonderful gift.

At first Grace was taken aback by the newest sober version of Caroline who seemed genuinely concerned about Grace's care. Twice before Grace had watched Caroline return fresh and optimistic from a stint in rehab only to fall down the rabbit hole again, yet this time Grace found herself slowly letting go of her fears and relaxing into the old friendship. Eventually Grace came to realize her long lost friend was back.

Caroline would push Grace in a wheelchair down to the solarium at the end of the hospital hallway where Caroline would sit in the May sunshine streaming through the windows and Grace would sit in the shade to protect her new skin. They spent hours in that sunny place reminiscing about their childhood and even talking about their futures.

On the day Caroline had the conversation with Charlie about Jack, she couldn't wait to get to Grace and tell her about it. She raced up the two flights of stairs to Grace's room, too excited to wait for the elevator. She rushed into the room, "Grace, you'll never believe what I just learned about Jack." The sight of Jack's mother, Kathryn, sitting in a chair next to Grace stopped Caroline in her tracks.

Caroline had given long and serious thought to how she could approach Kathryn, how she could mend their friendship, but in her wildest scenarios she never imagined they would meet again under these circumstances.

# 43

Neither Caroline nor Kathryn had discussed their rift with Grace, but Hedy and Annie discussed possible causes of the estrangement every time they visited Grace in the hospital.

Grace knew that whatever had happened must have been monumental since Kathryn was usually unshakeable in even the most difficult of circumstances. She also knew both of them well enough to suspect that if they were not discussing it with her than she must be involved somehow. Since Grace had nothing better to do with her time between physical therapy and skin grafts, she had given a great deal of thought to the situation and, coupled with Kathryn's badly hidden coldness toward James, she could think of only one possible secret that would turn Kathryn against Caroline so adamantly, but couldn't imagine how Kathryn had found out.

When Kathryn tried to initiate small talk the next time she stopped by the hospital for a visit, Grace was having none of it. "What's going on between you and Caroline?" she asked bluntly. "Nothing you need to think about," Kathryn replied. Grace realized that if the issue was what she thought it was, Kathryn would turn to stone before she would ever mention it to Grace, so she decided to tackle the problem head on.

"Does it involve James?" Grace asked candidly. Kathryn's loss of composure, however briefly, confirmed for Grace that her assumption was correct. "James? Of course not," Kathryn lied too slowly. "Kathryn, you have always been a terrible liar," Grace said with a smile. "Let me make this easy for you," Grace continued.

"I've known about their tryst for years. It happened the winter after the twins were born. Within a month of the 'event' Caroline came to my house one night so drunk I was shocked she was able to drive and blurted out all the sordid details. I had no doubt that what she told me was true and it became obvious to me as time went by that Caroline has no memory of that conversation. For weeks I considered all of the possible outcomes if I confronted James, until one day it dawned on me that I simply did not care. "

"I had just begun evening classes at Russell Sage working toward my master's degree and recognized divorce was a possible outcome of any conversation with James about Caroline. A divorce would bring with it all the legal headaches and detailed planning necessary to successfully raise three children living in two separate households, so I simply made a pragmatic decision to finish my degree first. I know it sounds shocking, Kathryn, but aside from the fact that he is the father of my children, learning about his tryst with Caroline, my best friend, was the proverbial last straw that broke the back of our marriage and left me with very little respect for the man."

"You remember what it's like raising three children, Kathryn, it's surprisingly easy to live in the same house with someone and avoid any real intimacy. That's the purgatory where I have been living for the past six years. It took two years to wrap up my masters, and by then the twins and Abigail required so much of my time and attention that it was simply easier to let sleeping dogs lie. Although I've always known the day would come when I would confront James and put our stumbling marriage out of its misery, I made no plans. That is until this happened." Grace said as she fluttered her hands down the front of her hospital gown.

She continued, "Having survived this horrible accident the fact that one's life can be taken away suddenly without warning is no longer a random truth of the universe. It is my first thought when I wake up and my last thought as I fall asleep at night." Tears began to spill out of Grace's eyes and she made no attempt to wipe them away as she stared into the eyes of her friend. "I am determined to live the life that is most meaningful to me, Kathryn, and that life does not include James. I've struggled during the past few months with the fear that no other man would want me with these scars until I realized I would not want any man that would be that shallow."

"My plan is this: once I have my health back, I will find a full-time teaching job and begin saving a nest egg to fall back on when the children and I are on our own. It's not that I don't trust James to contribute to the children's future; I'm simply not sure how successful he will be on his own. Are you shocked, Kathryn?"

"Yes, I am shocked, but, in all honesty, I am relieved that you see things so clearly. You know we are here for you if you need anything." "I do know that my friends will be there for me and that gives me courage."

"Now, about Caroline. How did you ever find out about her and James?"

Kathryn began the explanation in all seriousness, but as she continued the story of how she found Caroline's letter on her dining room table and pocketed it with the intention that James would read it to Grace, she could not stop from giggling when she heard the absurdity come out of her mouth. Grace was way ahead of her and holding her stomach as she roared with laughter.

The laughter had just died down when Caroline burst into the room claiming to have new information about Jack.

# 44

Admittedly, Kathryn's feelings toward Caroline had shifted in the previous 15 minutes. Now that she realized Grace had known all along about the night Caroline and James had spent together and that Grace had forgiven Caroline years ago, Kathryn felt hard-pressed to hold on to her own indignation. Unfortunately, she had no time to process those new feelings before Caroline burst into Grace's hospital room claiming to have news about Jack.

With her emotions split between her dissipating anger towards Caroline and her desire to hear more about her son, Kathryn asked Caroline what she was talking about, "What news do you have regarding Jack?" Grace sat with her mouth open, struck by the convergence of events unfolding in front of her.

As for Caroline, she was thunderstruck; first her conversation with Charlie about Jack and now this unanticipated confrontation with Kathryn. Standing there like a deer in the headlights Caroline began to slowly describe how she met Charlie, a man who actually knew Jack in Vietnam. She told them that Jack died in Laos, not Vietnam and after sitting down in a nearby chair, she explained how Jack's buddies wouldn't leave him behind and managed to get him back to Vietnam.

Grace spoke first breaking the silence, "What an amazing meeting, Caroline, and to think if you had not been involved in that accident, you probably never would have learned what happened to Jack." Both women turned toward Kathryn, who was sitting absolutely still except for her shoulders that moved in rhythm to the quiet sobbing sounds escaping from her mouth. Instinctively, Caroline stood up and walked toward the only other woman on the face of the earth that loved her Jack like she did. She knelt beside Kathryn and held her hand.

"Bless those young men that brought Jack home," Kathryn blurted out, "it was horrible enough losing Jack, but we would not have been able to endure if he was missing in action."

Fifteen minutes later, Hedy walked into that busy hospital room to find Kathryn and Caroline sitting next to each other in deep conversation, Grace sitting across from them with a silly smile on her face.

# 45

After 84 days in Albany Medical Center, the day finally arrived when it was time for Grace to go home. It rained that morning; a soft, persistent late-May rain that washed the dirt from the sidewalks and clung to the branches of the dogwood trees. Grace was overwhelmed by the simple pleasure of being outside after all that time in the medical center. What she remembered most from that morning was the smell of pure fresh spring air carrying a hint of wet dirt, the sweet aroma of flower buds about to burst, the unforgettable scent of fresh mown grass, and even the subtle smell of oil and gasoline drifting up from the wet pavement in the parking lot. It thrilled her and brought tears to her eyes. She had been inside far too long.

James settled Grace into the family car fussing more than was necessary but Grace didn't seem to notice. Her eyes couldn't drink in enough of the landscape as they drove through Albany's Washington Park where thousands of multi-colored tulips bloomed in well-groomed patches spread across the expansive lawns. The tulips reminded her of Albany's Annual Tulip Festival and she realized she had missed it by a few weeks. The festival was always held on Mother's Day weekend and she loved wandering around the park with the girls, eating vendor foods, and buying treasures from the craftspeople that set up canopies along the walkways. Next year, she thought.

The car left Albany behind and traveled over the Patroon Bridge spanning the Hudson River. Grace marveled at how the rain pelting the water's surface made the old river sparkle that morning. As they drove onto Washington Avenue in the City of Rensselaer, her eyes flitted from one well-cared-for cottage to the next until the landscape changed to open fields and she knew she was closer to home.

As the car pulled into their long driveway, Grace joked that they were approaching the scene of the crime, but her sweating palms reminded her of the apprehension she felt. A part of her was afraid to walk into the kitchen. Even though she had been told by James and others how the accident had happened, she had no memory of the events of that morning and didn't feel ready to relive them.

As they drove closer to the house, Grace was surprised and relieved to see Kathryn, Annie, and Hedy huddled together on the back porch out of the rain and she thanked heaven they were there.

After months of physical therapy Grace was capable of getting out of the car without help, although she did tend to favor her left knee, but on that morning she allowed her friends to support her. Even though she chatted and laughed with them as they approached the house, she couldn't take her eyes off of the kitchen door and she held her breath as they all burst into the room. To her relief no memories flashed, she simply felt the solace of being home and in the kitchen that she loved.

It wouldn't be until one cold morning the following winter, as she stood in the kitchen preparing breakfast for the girls and thinking about a project she would present to her second grade class later that morning that memories of how she was burned finally presented themselves. Fear, horror, and surprise flooded in with those memories and momentarily overwhelmed Grace. She stood still allowing the facts of the accident to sweep over her, then took a few deep breaths, and with trembling hands continued preparing breakfast until she felt two little arms wrap around her waist and a small head rest against her back. Without looking, she knew it was her dear sweet Abigail who had been so vigilant during her recovery. Smiling, Grace patted the little hands, whispered that she was okay and thanked the heavens that the moment she had feared for so long came bearing love.

# 46

Grace was glad she had insisted that the girls go to school the day she came home from the hospital. James left for work shortly after he dropped Grace at the house and he planned to jockey the girls to baseball practice and dance classes after school which meant they wouldn't be home until dinner time. Gracie's Tribe had filled the fridge with enough food to feed a small army for weeks so the friends had hours to sit around the kitchen table and catch up.

Although she had seen Annie a few times during the previous months, Grace couldn't keep her eyes off of her seven months pregnant friend. Grace was so used to seeing Annie in perpetual motion and wearing crisp business suits that watching the clearly relaxed version of Annie sitting across from her in a green and navy blue plaid maternity dress and navy blue flats was a revelation. Six weeks later Grace would be even more impressed when she stood beside Annie's bed in the maternity ward and saw Annie's beautiful daughter, Madeline Grace, for the first time. The new dad was proud to tell anyone who would listen that his lovely wife had weathered the birth as everyone expected, quickly and efficiently.

Later, watching Hedy talk with Kathryn, Grace thought Hedy looked ten years younger. Her face glowed with the look of someone who is well loved. Remembering the look of loss and wistfulness that always spread across Hedy's face whenever she spoke of Christopher, Grace could not help but love the man that had brought joy back into Hedy's life. But that's not the only reason why she loved Steven; he was the doctor that healed her. He always seemed to be at her side when she needed him the most. Sometimes he was more honest than she would have preferred, she smiled to herself, but always bringing hope and a confidence of purpose that nudged her forward.

A knock on the door interrupted Grace's thoughts and Caroline walked into the kitchen, breathless and apologizing for the late arrival. She had been at the hospital that morning. Dominick had a final surgery on his leg and the news was optimistic.

Annie watched Caroline accept a chair next to Kathryn and thought of the large financial settlement Caroline had insisted on giving to Dominick. She would have given him more but Dan and Annie talked her into a more sensible settlement which was still larger than any they had seen before. As Caroline's attorney, Annie was sworn to silence and couldn't share the details with anyone, but she did admire Caroline's new sense of responsibility.

Annie also knew about the college funds Caroline had created for Grace's three daughters and wondered if

Caroline had told Grace about the accounts yet. When the time came, the girls could attend any college of their choice without college loans hanging over their heads. Annie assumed Caroline set up those accounts as a gesture of fondness for her lifelong friend but, while it was true Caroline did love Grace like a sister, the real reason she had the trusts put in place was because Grace had confided in the "new" Caroline that she planned to end her marriage to James once she was back on her feet and Caroline did not want Grace taking out loans or worrying about college tuition when the girls were older.

During that same conversation Grace told a shocked Caroline that she knew she and James had slept together and that she forgave her. "I can't believe Kathryn told you about James," Caroline said incredulously when she heard the news. "It wasn't Kathryn," Grace responded with a smile on her face. "You told me right after it happened." Caroline's face dropped. "You came to my house late one night and confessed the whole thing." "And you've known all these years and still remained a good friend?" Caroline asked. "You were in such bad shape at that time, you didn't know what you were doing. James, on the other hand, has no such excuse. So that's the end of it, and we will never speak of it again."

All the members of Gracie's Tribe, including Caroline herself, were amazed by the sea change in Caroline's life since the accident. She quit drinking cold turkey and attended AA meetings several times a week. She finally moved forward on selling the monster of a house she lived in and it was sold within a week of the realtor's sign appearing on the front lawn. Rather than buying a condo, Caroline snapped up a small but charming cottage on Myrtle Avenue in Troy near Emma Willard School and near the neighborhood where she grew up. She took the things that mattered to her from the big house and hired an agent to sell off what remained.

The afternoon sun was dropping lower in the sky when Kathryn stood up and announced she had to get back to her shop for a six o'clock class and offered to prepare a meal. Hedy, Annie, and Caroline also decided to leave, but not before they all fussed around the stove leaving behind a steaming casserole. One final group hug and the five friends parted ways. Grace stood in her kitchen window watching her friends get into their cars and drive away.

She remained at the window looking out at the green fields and watching the yellow sky slowly change to shades of purple and pink until James and the girls drove up to the house. Seeing her three daughters jump out of the car almost before it came to a complete stop, and run up the porch steps toward her, Grace realized how happy she was to have the girls back in her daily life. She opened the door and let her daughters surround her, almost knocking her over, everyone happy mom was home again.

# Epilogue

## Seven years later

The black limo bumped slowly over the crumbling cemetery road although the occupants hardly noticed. Their eyes were on the funeral coach ahead of them carrying their friend and the first member of Gracie's Tribe to leave. On that clear and cold January morning they watched as the funeral coach took a right turn onto what looked like a charming country lane. Long rows of old maple trees stood at attention on either side of the narrow roadway as the morning sun peered through the bare branches. They were all thinking about an early spring morning 20 years before when smartly uniformed soldiers stood at attention beside their fallen comrade in that very cemetery.

The procession followed the pot-holed roadway for another three or four minutes before the funeral coach pulled off to the side. They watched from the warm limo as the pallbearers solemnly carried their friend across the brown lawn down the ten foot wide path that the groundskeeper had cleared in the newly fallen foot of snow, the same path they had walked before, leading to a spot they all knew too well.

After climbing out of the limo the four friends locked their arms together and reluctantly walked forward leaving everyone else to follow. As they got closer to the site they could see the young priest standing in the cold wind, his robes blowing behind him. They knew she would not have wanted a service, especially not a religious service, but they couldn't help themselves and gave in to their need to be sure that all of her bases were covered. No matter what she faced in the hereafter, she would be prepared.

The young man gave a lovely eulogy for the woman he did not know, incorporating some of the anecdotes her friends had shared with him. All things considered, they agreed in later conversations that he did an excellent job.

The priest's final words were barely out of his mouth when the indisputable sounds of a bagpipe began to drift through the air. Startled, everyone looked toward the sound and there stood a large man in a kilt and tam coaxing "Amazing Grace" from an old bagpipe; he was another of her many friends who had come to say goodbye. The remaining members of Gracie's Tribe looked at each other and almost laughed out loud knowing how much she would have hated those bagpipes.

When the serenade was over and the crowd began to slowly return to their cars, Gracie's Tribe walked the few steps to the other side of the tombstone so Kathryn could say hello to her son. Kathryn bent down and picked up three small pebbles that she used to build a tiny tower on the stone. It was a custom she began after reading that American Indians believed a soul could fly through the spaces in the stones and be free. Every time she visited Jack she left a tower, every time she returned it was gone.

"You probably know by now, Jack, that Caroline is on her way if you haven't seen her already," Kathryn began. "After the thousands of times she drove that car of hers so drunk she could barely see where she was going how ironic is it that she hadn't had a drink in years when she slid off the road in the snowstorm and hit that damned tree. We all miss her like crazy, Jack, but know that what she always wanted was to be with you again so our grief is tempered by the idea that you two are together. Take care of each other, sweetheart, until we meet again. I love you." Then three separate voices whispered behind her, "love you, too," "miss you," "love you Jack."

Smiling wearily at each other, the remaining members of Gracie's Tribe steeled themselves, locked arms again and walked away. One walking with a slightly discernable limp.

Everyone gathered at Grace's house after the services. Thanks to Annie's legal acumen Grace assumed sole ownership of the farmhouse after the divorce. Since it was the only home her girls had ever known, Grace fought hard to keep it.

That morning the twins, now 13 and freshmen in high school, had been babysitting Madeline Grace, or Maddie as everyone called her. Maddie, now 7 and in second grade, was a beauty and considered the twins her sisters which is why she was always following them around like a baby duckling.

Much to everyone's surprise, Annie stopped taking legal cases after Maddie was born and spent the next five years raising her daughter. Once Maddie was in school full-time, Annie accepted an offer from the Rensselaer County DA and became a part-time staff attorney. Not wanting to be left out of the fun, Dan sort of semi-retired after Maddie was born, working three-day weeks and living comfortably off his inheritance.

All of Grace's girls seemed to have weathered the divorce well. They even seemed to like James' new wife, a 25-year old woman he met at a pub near his bachelor apartment. Kathryn said they liked her because she was almost their own age. Annie called the new wife "James' mid-life crisis." Grace just smiled and felt relieved that James was someone else's problem now.

Abigail, now a 17-year old high school senior had just been accepted into Rensselaer Polytechnic Institute's Physician Scientist Program, a joint program with, of all places, Albany Medical College. In seven quick years, Abigail would be a full-fledged doctor. Grace believed Abigail chose the medical field because she was at such an impressionable age when Grace was scalded. Regardless of her reasons, Dr. Steven Devan was always impressed with Abigail's quick intellect and when she asked him to write a recommendation, he jumped at the chance creating such a stellar endorsement that he practically dared Albany Med to refuse her.

Grace was glad Abigail had chosen Rensselaer because it was only 15 miles away from the farmhouse. Even though she'd have to live on campus, at least she would be close.

Kathryn and John were sitting on the couch talking with Hedy and Steven. Grace could overhear snippets of their conversation and it sounded as though they were planning another trip. Two years before, to everyone's surprise, including Kathryn's, John sold his hardware store. Kathryn kept her shop, but spent less and less of her time there. She had never known that John had a desire to travel and see the world but that's what they were doing now when they weren't off visiting Frank and Tim and their four grandchildren.

Hedy and Steven had a comfortable life together. They never felt compelled to marry although they were obviously committed to each other. Since Steven retired from his medical practice they often traveled with Kathryn and John or you could find them relaxing at Steven's Syracuse farm where he renovated his family's old farmhouse and tore down most of the old buildings leaving nothing but miles of open fields. Often during the warm weather months Grace would pack up the girls on a weekend and make the two and a half hour drive to the farm where the girls ran around outside until they were exhausted and Grace, Hedy, Steven and Abigail as she got older, spent hours cooking, listening to music and sitting around discussing the problems of the world. Hedy still kept the Troy brownstone where they stayed when Steven was asked to consult on a medical case or when there was a long overdue meeting of the Tribe.

Grace led a busy life. Her parents were still alive and in good health. They were both in their late 80s residing in an assisted living facility a ten-minute drive from Grace's house. She was on the fast track to become the next principal of West Sand Lake Elementary School and when she wasn't with the girls, enjoyed an occasional night out with friends. She wasn't looking for a husband; she enjoyed the freedom of being single, but was open to possibilities.

Grace didn't think about the accident very often any more. Her doctors said she had made a complete recovery and for that she was grateful. However, every now and then, the small scars on her legs or abdomen would catch her attention and she'd run her fingers down the jagged ridges of skin remembering how her body had changed forever. Any sadness or regret that she felt was always fleeting, brushed away by the knowledge of how close she had come to losing the girls, her Tribe and this new life she had made for herself.